THE PANCH TATVA TALES: STORIES OF JOY AND WISDOM

AVNI CHATURVEDI

To my beloved mother, whose wisdom, love, and
encouragement planted the seed of this book in my heart.
Without you, this journey would never have begun.

To my family, friends, and relatives, who have been my
pillars of support and joy.

And to my best friends, who always believed in me and
stood by my side.

This book is a tribute to all of you—your love, support, and
belief in me have made this dream a reality.

Contents

Contents

FOREWORD

From the moment we take our first breath, we are surrounded by the five great elements—Earth, Water, Fire, Air, and Space. They are not just part of nature; they are our silent teachers, shaping our lives in ways we often do not realize.

In this book, we embark on a magical journey with a group of cousins as they discover the wisdom hidden within these elements. Through their adventures, they learn what it means to be strong like the Earth, adaptable like Water, passionate like Fire, free like Air, and limitless like Space.

This book is not just a collection of stories; it is an invitation—to children and adults alike—to see the world with new eyes, to find lessons in nature, and to embrace the wisdom that has been around us all along.

I hope these stories inspire you, make you smile, and remind you that the answers we seek are often hidden in the simplest things.

Happy reading!

PREFACE

The idea for this book was born from a simple yet profound conversation with my mother. Her words sparked a thought—what if the five elements, the very foundation of our existence, could teach us the most important lessons of life? What if children could learn kindness, courage, patience, and resilience not through lectures but through stories woven with adventure and fun?

This book is my attempt to bring that vision to life. It follows a group of cousins who, during their vacation, unknowingly step into a journey of self-discovery. Through everyday experiences, they come across lessons hidden in nature, guided by the wisdom of their grandmother and the world around them.

Writing this book has been a journey of love, learning, and gratitude. I hope it touches your heart as much as it has touched mine.

Acknowledgements

This book would not have been possible without the unwavering support and love of many people in my life.

First and foremost, to my mother, who gave me the very idea that blossomed into this book. Your guidance, encouragement, and belief in me have been my greatest strengths. Without your wisdom, this book would have remained just a dream.

To my family, friends, and relatives, who have cheered me on, listened to my ideas, and shared their thoughts, making this book even better.

To my best friends, who have been my source of encouragement, laughter, and motivation during this journey. Your faith in me has meant the world.

And lastly, to every reader, young or old, who picks up this book—I thank you. May these stories bring joy, wisdom, and inspiration into your life

PROLOGUE

In a small town, where the days were filled with laughter and the nights glowed under a sky full of stars, six cousins gathered at their grandparents' house for the summer. They thought this vacation would be like any other—full of games, fun, and adventure. But they had no idea that this time, they were about to embark on a journey of discovery, one that would change the way they saw the world.

Their wise Grandma held the key to a secret—hidden within nature itself. As she guided them through everyday experiences, she revealed the wisdom of the five elements. With every story she told, with every lesson she shared, the children began to see that nature was more than just trees, rivers, and skies—it was a teacher.

As they laughed, learned, and faced challenges together, they uncovered the greatest secret of all: the power of strength, kindness, patience, courage, and wisdom—the very essence of Earth, Water, Fire, Air, and Space.

And so, their adventure begans.............

I
Introduction

Welcome, Dear Reader!
Thank you for picking up this book. As you journey through these pages, may you discover the wisdom and magic hidden in the five elements—lessons that can guide us through life with strength, courage, and love.
I hope these stories inspire you, ignite your imagination, and fill your heart with wonder.
Enjoy the adventure!

Summer vacation was finally here, and the best part was about to begin—heading to Grandma's house! Grandma was so excited to see her four other grandchildren. Aditi and Shyam had already arrived the day before, and they couldn't wait for the rest of their cousins to join them.

The big day finally came! Srishti and Nandini, along with their parents, were on their way to Grandma's house! Grandpa, Aditi, and Shyam went to the airport to pick them up, and when they arrived, everyone was buzzing with excitement. Srishti and Nandini walked in with their suitcases, and as soon as they stepped inside, everyone shouted, "Grandma!" Grandma had been waiting eagerly for them, and she was so happy to see them. She had even taken a quick bath and put on her best clothes just for the occasion!

But wait—there were still two more cousins to come! The excitement grew as everyone waited for Alex and his big sister, Riddhi. Soon enough, they arrived with their parents, and the house was filled with even more giggles, smiles, and chatter.

Now, Grandma's house wasn't just a house anymore—it was full of joy and laughter from all the cousins. They couldn't wait to catch up with each other, so they started talking about everything—what happened at school, their friends, books they had read, places they had been to, and so much more! The air was full of curiosity, excitement, and fun, as the cousins spent time together, making memories they would cherish forever.

II

Beginning of The Stories

It was a warm summer afternoon at Grandma and Grandpa's house, the kind of afternoon that made everything feel slow and peaceful. The old house had a charm of its own, with its creaky wooden floors, shelves lined with ancient books that smelled like adventure, and the soft scent of Grandma's homemade sweets drifting in the air.

Outside, the sprawling garden was a little paradise of its own. Bright marigolds and roses nodded in the breeze, mango trees stood tall like gentle giants, and the little vegetable patch at the back was home to plump tomatoes and lazy cucumbers. Butterflies fluttered about, busy with their secret butterfly business, while birds chirped loudly as if gossiping about the latest news of the day.

Inside the house, in the cozy living room, the six cousins were sprawled across the floor, engaged in a very serious discussion. Well, at least, Aditi thought it was serious. The others were mostly lying around like sleepy kittens, thanks to the extra bowl of mango ice cream they had begged Grandpa for after lunch.

"Guys," Aditi began, brushing her long braid over her shoulder. "I've been thinking about something."

"Uh-oh," Alex groaned, stretching like a lazy cat. "That sounds dangerous."

Aditi saw him in a angry look and then looked at others and continued, "Before the holidays, my teacher gave us an assignment—to talk about what makes a person truly good. We were supposed to think about it over the break. But honestly, I have no idea where to start!"

At this, the others perked up.

"What do you mean by 'truly good'?" Shyam asked, rolling onto his stomach and propping his chin up with his hands.

"Our teacher said that being good is not just about saying nice things or following rules. It's something deeper. But I don't understand what that means," Aditi admitted.

"Being good means listening to your parents," Riddhi suggested.

"It means sharing your toys!" Srishti added.

"Or helping others," Nandini chimed in.

"But sometimes, I don't feel like sharing," Alex said. "And sometimes, I get angry or upset. Does that mean I'm not good?"

The room fell silent. Nobody had an answer.

Then, suddenly—

"Let's ask Grandma!" Shyam said excitedly, jumping up so fast that he knocked over a cushion. "She always has the best explanations!"

Everyone nodded. That was a brilliant idea. Grandma always knew everything. Whether it was the secret to making the perfect cup of hot cocoa, why the moon changes shape, and many of the secrets!

So, off they went, racing down the hallway in a chaotic stampede.

"Ow! Watch where you're stepping, Alex!"

"Hey! Who pushed me?"

"Shyama! That was my foot!"

They tumbled into the sunlit veranda, where Grandma sat in her favorite rocking chair, peacefully knitting a soft shawl for winter. She looked up and smiled as the children gathered around her like a flock of noisy birds.

"Grandmaaaa!" they all called out at once.

She chuckled, her eyes twinkling like stars. "What is it, my little ones?"

Aditi stepped forward, still catching her breath. "Grandma, we need your help. How do we know what makes a person truly good?"

Grandma put down her knitting and leaned forward. "Ah, that is a wonderful question!" She added, "But before I answer, tell me—what do you all think?"

The children launched into a storm of answers.

"Kindness!"

"Honesty!"

"Sharing!"

"Listening to elders!"

"Not fighting with siblings!" (At this every sibling looked at each other and smiled)

Grandma smiled. "All of those things are important. But let me ask you—do you always feel like doing the right thing?"

The children hesitated.

"Sometimes, I get too lazy to help," Shyam admitted.

"And I get jealous when someone else gets something nice," Srishti murmured.

"See? Being good isn't just about knowing what's right—it's about learning how to be right, even when it's difficult," Grandma said gently.

"Then how do we learn it, Grandma?" Riddhi asked.

Grandma's smile grew wider. "My dears, the answers are all around us—in nature itself! The five great elements—Earth, Water, Fire, Air, and Space—each teach us something valuable about being a better person. They have been guiding people for centuries. If you learn from them, you will understand what it means to truly be good."

The cousins sat up, intrigued.

"Really? How can things like water and air teach us about being good?" Alex asked skeptically.

Grandma laughed. "Patience, little one! You will see soon enough. Tomorrow, as you play, travel, and experience different things, nature will begin to teach you. Watch closely, and you will understand."

Before anyone could ask more, Grandpa's voice called from the kitchen:

"Everyone, lunch is ready!"

At this, the cousins forgot all about their deep discussion and raced to the dining table, nearly tripping over each other in excitement.

A Feast to Remember

Lunch was a grand affair. There was a steaming plate of noodles, a giant bowl of pasta, crispy golden pooris with Grandma's special mango pickle, and the best part—Grandpa's famous homemade mango ice cream, made from the fruit of his own tree.

"More ice cream, please!" Alex pleased, waving his spoon like a flag.

Grandpa chuckled. "Only if you promise not to complain about your belly aching later!"

"I promise!" Alex grinned. (It was a lie. He would definitely complain later.)

After stuffing themselves until they could barely move, the cousins lounged in the sunlit room, their eyes drooping lazily. Through the big glass doors that led to the garden, they could see the mighty mango tree, its leaves dancing in the breeze.

Soon, their mothers packed their bags, preparing to return to the city for very urgent work as Unfortunately they did not got any holidays(They all had a job). The children hugged them tightly before watching Grandpa drive them to the station in his big white car.

That night, the cousins found themselves full of excitement, yet still thinking about Grandma's words.

"Do you think we'll really learn from nature?" Srishti whispered as they lay in their beds.

"I don't know," Aditi replied, staring at the ceiling, "but I want to find out!"

Finally, Grandma who was litening to them, smiled and tucked them into bed. "Sleep well, my children. Tomorrow, your journey of learning will begin!!."

As the night deepened, the cousins drifted off to sleep, their dreams filled with the mysteries of the five great elements, waiting to reveal their lessons...

III

The Secret Within The Earth

The next morning, the cousins woke up to the smell of freshly made parathas drifting through the house. The golden rays of the sun streamed in through the windows, casting a warm glow on their sleepy faces. Shyam stretched lazily. "Mmm... nothing wakes me up like the smell of Grandma's cooking!"

Alex groaned. "I was having such a nice dream. I was a knight fighting a dragon! But now my stomach is growling louder than the dragon."

The others giggled as they hurried to wash up and rush to the dining table. Grandma was already serving hot, buttered parathas with sweet mango chutney and yogurt. Grandpa sat at the head of the table, reading the newspaper, but the moment the kids sat down, he peered over the top of his glasses. "So, what's on today's adventure list? Climbing Mount Pillow in the bedroom? Wrestling with the mighty Blanket Monster?"

The children laughed, shaking their heads. "No, Grandpa! We're going to the park today!" Aditi said.

"Ohh, the park! Good choice." Grandpa nodded approvingly. "Just don't get stuck on top of the jungle gym again, Shyam. Remember last time?"

Shyam turned red as everyone burst out laughing. "That was one time! And the ladder was shaky!"

"Of course, of course," Grandpa teased with a twinkle in his eye. "Eat well, young adventurers. You'll need your strength!"

After breakfast, they packed their water bottles and a small bag of snacks and headed to the park. The sun was bright, the air smelled of fresh grass, and the laughter of other children echoed around them.

"Let's have a race!" Shyam announced, pointing towards the jungle gym.

"You're on!" Alex grinned, tightening his shoelaces.

Meanwhile, on the soft patch of sand, Aditi and Nandini were busy building what they claimed would be the grandest sandcastle the park had ever seen.

Srishti and Riddhi soon joined in, shaping towers and carving out small windows. They worked together, smoothing the walls and decorating the castle with tiny pebbles they found nearby.

"This is looking amazing!" Nandini said, stepping back to admire their work.

"I think we should add a moat around it," Riddhi suggested, dragging her fingers through the sand to create a small trench.

Srishti clapped her hands. "Yes! And we can put some twigs on top as a flag."

Their castle was almost complete, standing tall and beautiful, as if it belonged in a fairy tale.

Just then, a strong gust of wind blew through the park. Before anyone could react, the castle collapsed, crumbling into a pile of loose sand.

"Oh no!" Srishti gasped. "All our hard work... gone in seconds!"

Nandini crossed her arms, frowning at the ruined castle. "This isn't fair. We worked so hard on it!"

Riddhi sighed. "Maybe we should just go play something else..."

At that moment, Grandma, who had been sitting on a nearby bench, watching them, stood up and walked over. She smiled and gently placed her hand on Srishti's shoulder.

"My dear children," she said warmly, "do you know what this reminds me of?"

The cousins looked at her curiously.

"What, Grandma?" Aditi asked.

Grandma pointed to the ground beneath their feet. "Look at this earth. No matter how many times we step on it, dig into it, or even fall, the earth stays strong. It never complains, never wobbles, and always supports us."

Srishti furrowed her brows. "But what does that have to do with our castle?"

Grandma chuckled. "Think about it. Your castle was built on loose sand, without a strong foundation. A little wind came, and it couldn't stand. But what if you build something on solid ground, something strong like the earth beneath us?"

The boys who were listening got alerted that Grandma was about to tell a story and ran towards her.

As the sun set behind the trees, painting the sky in hues of orange and pink, the cousins gathered around Grandma on a wooden bench in the park. The warm breeze rustled the leaves, and the scent of fresh earth filled the air.

"Grandma," Srishti asked, still feeling a little upset about their sandcastle, "You always tell us stories. Can you tell us one now?"

Grandma chuckled and nodded. "Of course, my dear. This story is about a young sapling named Bhoomi."

The children sat up eagerly, their curiosity piqued.

The Story of Bhoomi, the Little Tree

A long time ago, in a peaceful village, a tiny banyan sapling named Bhoomi sprouted beside a riverbank. She was small, delicate, and swayed easily with the wind.

One day, Bhoomi saw a tall coconut tree nearby, standing strong and proud. "Wow, I wish I could be tall and strong like him," Bhoomi sighed.

The coconut tree heard her and laughed. "Little one, if you want to be strong, you need deep roots. When the storms come, weak trees fall, but those with deep roots stand firm."

Bhoomi nodded but didn't quite understand.

As months passed, she continued to grow, stretching her branches toward the sky. But she noticed something—whenever strong winds blew, the small plants around her got uprooted. Bhoomi trembled too, but her roots were holding her steady.

Then came a terrible storm. Dark clouds covered the sky, and heavy rain poured down. The wind howled like a wild beast, bending and breaking small plants. Bhoomi struggled, feeling the force of the storm shake her to the core.

"I will not fall! I must hold on!" she whispered, gripping the earth with all her strength.

The coconut tree swayed violently but remained standing. Bhoomi watched as trees with weak roots got uprooted. Some fell into the river, others crashed to the ground. She feared she might be next.

But something amazing happened—her roots dug even deeper into the earth, and though she bent with the wind, she did not break.

When the storm finally passed, Bhoomi stood tall, stronger than before. She had learned the secret—the deeper the roots, the stronger the tree. Over time, she grew into a mighty banyan tree, providing shelter to birds, animals, and tired travelers.

And from then on, whenever a storm came, she never feared it. She embraced it, knowing she was unshakable.

ॐ

Grandma finished the story, looking at the children with a gentle smile. "Do you see, my little ones? Just like Bhoomi, life will bring storms—challenges, failures, and disappointments. But if we have deep roots—patience, strength, and determination—we will never fall."

Aditi nodded thoughtfully. "So, when we face problems, instead of giving up, we should become stronger inside?"

"Exactly," Grandma said, beaming.

Srishti smiled, glancing at their sandcastle. "I guess we should have built our foundation better, just like Bhoomi!"

Grandma patted her head. "And just like Bhoomi, whenever life shakes you, remember—real happiness is knowing that no matter what comes, you can stand strong."

As the park lights flickered on, the cousins sat silently, absorbing the wisdom of the story. The sandcastle was just a small lesson, but what they had learned today would stay with them forever.

Lesson from Earth: Happiness comes from inner strength. Just like the earth holds everything firm, we must be steady and strong to withstand life's storms.

Grandma smiled and said "And this time, make the base stronger. Press the sand tightly, make it firm, and your castle will stand much longer."

Inspired by Grandma's words, the cousins started rebuilding. This time, they packed the sand tightly, pressing it down before adding the towers. They worked with patience, learning from their mistakes.

Finally, after a long effort, the castle stood tall once again.

"This one is even better than before!" Srishti grinned.

"And stronger!" Riddhi added, patting the sand.

IV

Flow Like Water: Srishti's Perfect Choice

It was the next day. The weather seemed perfect for shopping today, and so all of them got ready and they sat into the big old White car of Grandpa and went on a ride to the mall. Grandma and Grandpa told them that today, whichever clothes they want, they can choose them as a gift from their Grandparents. Finally, they reached to a grand, famous mall which was too huge.

The glass doors slid open with a soft whoosh, revealing a world full of colors, lights, and endless choices. It was the perfect day for shopping.

The mall was buzzing with excitement—families laughing, shopkeepers arranging displays, and the sweet aroma of popcorn and chocolates filling the air.

It was the perfect day for shopping, and the excitement among the kids was undeniable.

"Where should we go first?" Alex asked, smiling with joy

"The biggest clothing store, of course!" Aditi grinned.

With that, the children rushed inside, their eyes widening at the dazzling display of dresses, jackets, t-shirts, and accessories. The store was filled with bright fabrics and trendy designs, making it hard to choose just one.

"Look at this one!" Aditi said, holding up a pink dress with shiny sequins. She twirled it playfully.

"This jacket is awesome," Alex grinned, trying on a black leather one.

"Ugh, that's too grown-up," Nandini teased, picking up a flowy yellow-purple dress.

One by one, the kids picked their favorite clothes, laughing and discussing which outfit looked best. But in the middle of all this excitement, Srishti stood quietly, her arms crossed, scanning the shelves with a frown.

"What's wrong, Srishti?" Riddhi asked.

"I don't like any of these," Srishti mumbled.

"That's okay! Let's check another store," Aditi suggested.

So, they left and entered another shop. The display was different—more stylish, more trendy—but again, Srishti shook her head.

Store after store, they searched. Some had traditional clothes, others had funky modern designs. Still, nothing made Srishti's eyes sparkle with joy.

"Come on, Srishti, just pick something," Shyam groaned, exhausted from walking.

"I don't want to pick just anything," she sighed. "It has to feel right."

The group finally sat down on a bench near the food court, tired from walking. Srishti let out a deep sigh. "Maybe I should just buy something randomly. Everyone else found something, but I still have nothing."

Grandpa, who had been watching them patiently, chuckled softly. "Children, you all can order whatever you want to eat" Everyone ordered Pizzas, Burgers, Noodles, French Fries, and ice cream, each with different flavours that the children liked. Grandma, who was observing Srishti's annoyance, smiled and said, "Come on, Srishti, you are my big girl. Come, let me tell you all, one more story among those 5 elements while we are waiting for the food to come."

Once upon a time, high up in the mountains, a little stream was born. She bubbled with excitement, eager to find her place in the world.

"I must hurry! I need to find where I truly belong!" she told herself as she rushed down the hills.

First, she reached a rocky cliff. "Maybe I should stop here," she thought. But when she tried, she realized she couldn't—her waters spilled over the edge, forming a waterfall.

"This isn't right," she sighed and kept moving.

Next, she flowed into a dry desert. "Maybe this is where I'm meant to stay!" she said, trying to spread herself across the sand. But the hot sun drank up her water too quickly.

Feeling lost, the little stream kept flowing, searching for the perfect place.

Then, after a long journey, she reached a peaceful valley where trees, flowers, and animals were waiting for her. Without thinking, she settled in, forming a calm, beautiful river. The birds chirped happily, the trees stretched their roots to drink, and the people rejoiced.

"This is it!" she smiled. "I didn't choose this place—it chose me!"

And from that day on, the river understood: just like water, we don't have to force things. If we keep flowing, life will naturally take us where we are meant to be.

ॐ

Back to the Mall

Srishti's eyes lit up as she listened. "So, I shouldn't force myself to pick something? I should just... go with the flow?"

Grandma nodded. "Exactly, my dear Srishti. Water doesn't struggle—it finds its way naturally."

Srishti smiled, feeling lighter. "Okay! Let's keep looking. I'll just enjoy the search instead of stressing."

Grandpa stopped them, and then Srishti looked towards him in a doubtful and sad face, thinking she would not be allowed to take any clothes for herself anymore.

Grandpa smiled and said, "Won't you eat this yummy food you have ordered?" Everybody laughed, and after their lunch break, Srishti and her cousins told her to help her choose one, and then they went to another store.

And just like the river, when she stopped worrying, she finally found the perfect gown with sparkling stars, one she hadn't noticed before, but as soon as she saw it, she knew it was the one.

That day, Srishti didn't just buy a dress. She learned the secret to happiness—when we stop forcing and start flowing, the right things come to us.

Everybody was very happy and joyful, eagering when to wear it, sat in the car, and joyfully discussed about their clothes.

Then, like usual, they ate their dinner and went to sleep, waiting for the next adventurous day to come when they again could get the opportunity to learn something new!!............................

Shopping mall

V
Trip to Hill

The morning after their stargazing adventure, the cousins woke up feeling refreshed and full of energy. Sunlight streamed through the windows, and a cool breeze rustled the curtains. Birds chirped outside, and the scent of fresh flowers drifted into the room.

Aditi stretched and yawned. "That was the best sleep ever!"

"Yeah," Shyam agreed, rubbing his eyes. "And did you guys notice how breezy it is today? It feels so nice!"

Grandma, who had just entered the room with a tray of hot milk and biscuits, smiled. "That's because the air is happy today."

"Happy?" Alex asked, grabbing a biscuit. "How can air be happy?"

Grandma chuckled. "Air is always around us, but we don't always notice it. It moves freely, bringing coolness on hot days and carrying the scent of flowers. It never holds onto anything; it just flows. And that's what makes it so light and joyful."

The cousins looked at each other.

"I like the air when it's cool," Nandini said. "But when it's too windy, it messes up my hair!"

Everyone laughed.

"That's because air teaches us something very important," Grandma said. "It reminds us to be light, free, and not to hold onto things too tightly. Sometimes, we take life too seriously and forget to enjoy the little moments."

"But how do we learn that?" Srishti asked, munching on a biscuit.

"Well," Grandma said with a twinkle in her eye, "perhaps today will teach you."

A Trip to the Hill

Just then, Grandpa walked in, whistling cheerfully. "Kids! Guess what? My old friend who runs the paragliding center on the hill invited us for a visit! How about we go for an adventure?"

"Paragliding?" the cousins gasped in unison.

"Yes!" Grandpa grinned. "Even if you don't want to fly, it's a beautiful place with open skies and fresh air. Perfect for a picnic."

The cousins cheered. Within an hour, they packed snacks, water bottles, and sunglasses, and set off in Grandpa's jeep.

The drive up the hill was breathtaking. The road twisted through green valleys, and as they climbed higher, the air became cooler and fresher. When they finally reached the top, they gasped.

The hilltop was vast and open, with a perfect view of the endless sky. Below, they could see a winding river, tiny houses, and golden fields stretching into the horizon.

"Wow," Riddhi whispered. "It feels like we're on top of the world!"

In the distance, people were paragliding—floating gently in the air with colorful parachutes. The cousins watched in awe as the flyers soared like birds.

"I want to try!" Shyam announced.

"I don't know..." Nandini hesitated. "It looks scary."

Just then, a friendly instructor approached. "Would you like to try tandem paragliding? It's completely safe, and you'll be flying with an expert."

Shyam and Alex were excited, but the others weren't sure.

"I think I'll just watch," Aditi said.

"Me too," Nandini added.

"Why are you scared?" Shyam teased. "It's just air!"

"That's the problem!" Riddhi laughed. "Air doesn't have anything to hold onto!"

Grandma, who had been quietly observing, smiled. "Ah, my dear ones. That's exactly what air teaches us. It teaches us to trust, to let go of fear, and to enjoy the ride."

"But it's hard!" Aditi admitted. "What if something goes wrong?"

Grandma chuckled. "That reminds me of a story."

The cousins, always excited for a story, quickly gathered around as Grandma began.

The Story of Vayu, the Little Breeze

Long ago, in a land surrounded by mountains, there lived a little breeze named Vayu. He was playful and light, dancing through the trees and bringing coolness to the people.

But Vayu had one problem—he was afraid to fly too high.

"What if I get lost in the sky?" he would worry. "What if I disappear?"

So, while all the other winds soared freely over the valleys, Vayu stayed close to the ground, never daring to rise.

One day, an old wise eagle called Garuda saw Vayu and asked, "Why don't you fly high like the others?"

"I'm scared," Vayu admitted. "What if I fall? What if I lose control?"

Garuda chuckled. "My dear breeze, do you know why the wind is so free?"

Vayu shook his head.

"Because it doesn't hold onto anything," Garuda said. "It trusts the sky, moves with ease, and simply enjoys the journey. That is what makes it joyful."

Vayu listened carefully.

"Try it once," Garuda encouraged. "Just let go and trust yourself."

Taking a deep breath, Vayu gathered his courage. He let go of his fear and started to rise—higher, higher, and higher. For the first time, he felt truly free.

He danced across the sky, twirling between clouds, brushing against mountaintops, and bringing coolness to villages far and wide. He realized that the more he let go, the lighter and happier he became.

From that day on, Vayu was no longer afraid. He became the wind that brought laughter to children, carried the scent of flowers, and whispered secrets to the trees.

And most importantly, he learned that true joy comes from letting go.

Back at the Hilltop

ॐ

As Grandma finished, the cousins sat in thoughtful silence.

"So, Vayu learned to let go of fear and enjoy the ride?" Aditi said slowly.

"Exactly," Grandma nodded. "And that's what Air teaches us. We hold onto worries, fears, and grudges, but sometimes, we just need to let go and trust life."

Shyam grinned. "Well, I'm going to be like Vayu. I'm flying!"

With that, he ran toward the instructor, eager to try paragliding. Alex soon followed.

The others still hesitated, but as they watched their brothers glide smoothly in the air, they felt a little braver.

Finally, Riddhi took a deep breath. "Alright. If Air can be free, so can I."

One by one, the cousins took turns flying. Some screamed at first, but soon, they laughed, feeling the wind rush past them, carrying them like birds in the sky.

Even Aditi, who had been the most nervous, found herself smiling as she floated weightlessly.

"This is amazing!" she shouted. "I feel so light!"

"Yes," the instructor laughed. "That's because you've let go of fear. The sky holds you, just like the air does."

Grandma and Grandpa watched from below, smiling proudly.

The Lesson from Air

When they returned home, the cousins sat together in the garden, still feeling the thrill of their flight.

"You know," Srishti said, "Air is really special. It's always moving, never stuck, never worrying too much. Maybe we should be like that too."

"Yes," Grandma agreed. "Air reminds us to be lighthearted, to let go of things we cannot control, and to trust the journey of life."

"Like when we get upset over small things," Nandini added. "Instead, we should just breathe and move on."

Grandma nodded. "And that, my dear ones, is why Air is so joyful. Because it is free."

The cousins smiled, feeling lighter than ever.

That night, as they lay in bed, they could still feel the wind against their cheeks. They closed their eyes and let go of all their worries, knowing that just like Air, they too could be free.

VI

Fire – Passion and Courage

The next morning, the sun filtered through the curtains of Grandma and Grandpa's house, casting a warm glow over the room where the cousins lay sprawled on their beds. Some were still fast asleep, while others blinked groggily at the ceiling, reluctant to leave the cozy embrace of their blankets.

The house was filled with the comforting aroma of fresh parathas sizzling on the stove and the sweet, familiar scent of cardamom-flavored tea. The distant hum of Grandpa's old radio played a lively tune, signaling the start of another beautiful day.

"Wake up, everyone!" Aditi stretched her arms, rubbing her sleepy eyes. "What's the plan for today?"

Shyam yawned. "I don't think there is a plan."

The others groaned in disappointment. The previous day had been exciting, with their shopping trip to the mall, but now it seemed like they had nothing to look forward to.

Just then, there was a loud honk from outside.

"Who could that be so early in the morning?" Riddhi wondered, peeking through the window.

Before anyone could guess, Grandpa's cheerful voice boomed through the house. "Look who's here, kids!"

Curious, the cousins rushed to the veranda, where they saw an elderly man with twinkling eyes and a broad smile stepping out of an old blue scooter. He had salt-and-pepper hair, a slightly round belly, and wore a crisp white kurta.

"Uncle Ramesh!" Grandma greeted warmly.

The children looked at each other in confusion.

"Who's Uncle Ramesh?" Alex whispered.

Grandpa chuckled. "Ramesh is my best friend! We've known each other since we were your age. And guess what? He has some exciting news for you all!"

Ramesh smiled and patted Grandpa on the back. "You haven't changed a bit, old friend!" Then, turning to the children, he said, "I've come to invite you all to the fair that I've organized near my house! It's a special event with lots of games, rides, and delicious food!"

"A fair?!" the cousins exclaimed in unison, their previous boredom instantly forgotten.

"Yes!" Ramesh laughed. "It's happening today, and I thought—who better to enjoy it than you little ones? So, what do you say? Will you come?"

The answer was obvious.

"Of course!" Nandini grinned.

"This is going to be the best day ever!" Srishti clapped her hands.

Grandpa nodded. "Then let's not waste any time! Finish your breakfast, and we'll head to the fair!"

The children quickly rushed to the dining table, stuffing their mouths with Grandma's delicious parathas and mango chutney, eager to begin their adventure.

The Fair and the Game of Determination

The fair was bustling with energy—colorful stalls lined the streets, music played from large speakers, and the aroma of spicy chaat and fresh jalebis filled the air. There were all kinds of rides—a Ferris wheel that reached high into the sky, a spinning teacup ride, and even a small train chugging along a track.

The cousins were thrilled. They ran from one stall to another, trying different snacks and playing games.

"This is amazing!" Shyam shouted as they rode the giant Ferris wheel, their laughter mixing with the joyful screams of other children.

Then, as they wandered through the fair, they spotted a game stall.

"Look!" Nandini pointed. "It's a ring toss game!"

A large teddy bear sat on the counter as the grand prize, its fluffy fur gleaming under the fair's bright lights.

Alex's eyes gleamed with excitement. "I want to win that!"

He stepped forward, picked up a ring, and aimed carefully. He threw it—but it missed.

"It's okay," Riddhi encouraged. "Try again!"

Alex threw another ring, and then another, but they all kept missing. His confidence began to fade.

"This game is impossible," he muttered. "It's rigged!"

"Come on, Alex," Aditi said. "You just have to keep trying!"

But Alex shook his head. "What's the point? I'll never win."

Just then, Grandma, who had been watching from a nearby bench, walked over with a knowing smile.

"My dear Alex," she said gently, "do you know what this reminds me of?"

The cousins immediately perked up. They knew Grandma was about to tell them a story.

"What, Grandma?" Alex asked, frowning.

Grandma settled onto a wooden bench near the game stall and gestured for them to sit around her. As the lights of the fair twinkled around them, she began her story.

The Story of Agni, the Little Flame

Long ago, in a small village, there lived a tiny flame named Agni. Agni was born from a spark in the village's fire pit. He was small and weak, flickering whenever the wind blew.

One day, the villagers gathered to prepare for a grand festival, and Agni was supposed to help light the lamps. But each time he tried to burn brightly, the wind would blow him out.

"I'm too small," Agni sighed. "I'll never be a strong fire."

Nearby, an old bonfire crackled warmly. "Do you know what makes a fire strong?" the bonfire asked.

Agni shook his head.

"It's not about how big you are," the bonfire said. "It's about how much passion you have inside. Fire never gives up. The more you believe in yourself, the stronger you burn."

"But I keep failing!" Agni protested.

The bonfire smiled. "Failure is just fuel. Every time you fail, you learn, and that makes your flame burn brighter."

Agni thought for a moment. Then, instead of giving up, he tried again. This time, when the wind came, he leaned into it, burning stronger instead of fading.

Little by little, Agni grew. He became a bright, powerful fire, lighting all the lamps for the festival. From that day on, Agni never feared the wind—because he knew that as long as he kept his passion alive, he would never go out.

⌘

Grandma finished the story, looking at Alex with a kind smile.

"You see, my dear," she said, "fire never stops burning just because the wind tries to put it out. It fights back, grows stronger, and shines even brighter. Passion and determination keep the fire alive."

Alex sat quietly, thinking about the story.

"So... I should keep trying?" he asked.

Grandma nodded. "Every time you fail, you learn. And every time you learn, you get better. That's how you win—not just in games, but in life."

Alex's frustration melted away. He stood up and faced the game stall again.

"I want to try one more time," he said.

He took a deep breath, focused, and threw the first ring. It missed.

But he didn't give up.

He threw the second ring—it landed just outside the target.

On his last attempt, he remembered Agni's lesson. With determination burning inside him, he aimed carefully and threw the final ring.

It landed perfectly on the bottle!

"You did it, Alex!" the cousins cheered.

The stall owner smiled and handed him the big teddy bear. Alex hugged it, grinning.

"I guess I just needed to keep my fire alive!" he said happily.

As the cousins walked through the fair, enjoying cotton candy and talking excitedly, Alex kept his teddy bear close, knowing that it wasn't just a prize—it was a reminder of the lesson Fire had taught him.

Lesson from Fire:

Passion and perseverance keep the spirit alive. Just like fire never gives up, we must keep trying and believing in ourselves, no matter how many times we fail.

That night, as they returned home, tired but happy, Alex whispered to himself before falling asleep:

"I won't give up so easily anymore. My fire will always burn bright."

VII

Space – Openness, Acceptance, and Wisdom

After their exciting day at the fair, the cousins slept deeply, exhausted but content. The next morning, they woke up to a peaceful and quiet atmosphere. The sky was a soft shade of blue, dotted with wispy clouds, and a cool breeze drifted through the open windows of Grandma and Grandpa's house.

As they gathered in the veranda for breakfast, sipping warm milk and munching on toast with Grandma's homemade jam, Shyam stretched his arms and sighed.

"I feel like we've learned something from every element now," he said.

"Yeah!" Srishti agreed. "Earth taught us strength, Water showed us adaptability, Fire showed us passion, and Air reminded us to be lighthearted and free. I feel like we're so much wiser already!"

"But wait," Aditi suddenly frowned. "Isn't there one element left?"

They all paused, looking at each other.

"Space!" Riddhi exclaimed.

"That's right," Grandma said, walking in with a knowing smile. "You have learned from four elements, but there is still one more that holds them all together—Space."

"But what can Space teach us?" Alex wondered. "I mean, it's just... empty, right?"

Grandma chuckled. "Oh, my dear, Space is not just emptiness. It is vast, infinite, and holds everything within it—without complaining, without rejecting, and without trying to control. It teaches us to be open, to accept, and to see the bigger picture in life."

The cousins looked at each other, still a little puzzled.

"Maybe you will understand better when the time is right," Grandma said mysteriously. "Now, what's the plan for today?"

"Uhh... there is no plan," Shyam admitted.

"We've already done so much—playing, shopping, the fair... What else is left?" Nandini sighed.

Just then, Grandpa walked in, holding an envelope in his hand.

"You might want to rethink that, kids!" he said with a mischievous smile.

The cousins sat up, curious.

"What is it, Grandpa?" Srishti asked.

"This," he said, waving the envelope, "is an invitation to a stargazing night at the planetarium! My friend, who works there, sent it just for you kids. It's happening tonight!"

The cousins gasped in excitement.

"A night under the stars?" Aditi squealed.

"That sounds amazing!" Riddhi beamed.

Grandpa nodded. "And not just that—there will be a special session where they will show you how vast and endless the universe really is."

"Whoa..." Alex whispered. "That sounds... HUGE."

"Because it is," Grandma said with a twinkle in her eye. "And perhaps, that's where you'll find your lesson from Space."

A Night Under the Stars

That evening, after an early dinner, the cousins set off for the planetarium with Grandma and Grandpa. The planetarium was a large, dome-shaped building, and as they stepped inside, they were greeted by a scientist who led them into a special viewing hall.

"Welcome, young explorers!" the scientist said warmly. "Tonight, you will witness something magical—the vastness of the universe!"

The lights dimmed, and suddenly, the ceiling transformed into a breathtaking night sky. Thousands of twinkling stars appeared above them, stretching endlessly in every direction. The children gasped in awe.

"It's so... big," Nandini whispered.

"Indeed," the scientist said. "Space is infinite. No matter how much we explore, there will always be more to discover."

As they watched in amazement, constellations formed, planets spun, and galaxies swirled like glowing whirlpools.

"Do you see how everything has a place in space?" Grandma whispered to them. "The stars don't fight for space. The planets don't complain that they're too far or too close. Space holds them all, allowing everything to exist as it is."

The cousins listened carefully.

"Space teaches us acceptance," Grandma continued. "It reminds us that everyone and everything has a place in this world. Just like space holds the stars, we must also learn to hold love, kindness, and wisdom in our hearts, without pushing others away."

The cousins exchanged glances.

"That makes sense," Riddhi said thoughtfully. "Sometimes, I get annoyed when things don't go my way. But maybe I should just... accept them, like Space does."

"Exactly," Grandma nodded. "Space teaches us to be open—to new ideas, to people's differences, and to the vastness of life."

"But wait," Shyam said, still gazing up at the stars. "If Space is so big, doesn't that make us... really small?"

"Ah," Grandma smiled. "That's the beauty of it. Space reminds us how tiny we are in this universe, yet how important we are too. Even a single star, though small, can shine bright enough to guide someone in the dark."

The cousins sat in silence for a while, letting the lesson sink in.

The Lesson from Space

When the show ended, the children stepped outside, looking up at the real night sky. The vast, endless expanse of stars twinkled above them, stretching far beyond what their eyes could see.

"I think I finally understand," Aditi said softly. **"Space teaches us to be open, to accept everything as it is, and to see the bigger picture."**

"Yeah," Srishti added. "Like, sometimes, we get upset over small things. But in the grand scheme of life, those problems aren't as big as they seem."

"And just like stars need space to shine," Alex said, "we need to give people space too—to grow, to learn, and to be themselves."

Grandma smiled proudly. "Exactly, my little ones. You have now learned from all five elements."

As they walked back home under the endless sky, a peaceful feeling settled over them. They felt lighter, wiser, and more connected to the world around them.

That night, as they lay in bed, staring at the stars through the window, they understood something truly special—

Like Space, they too could be vast in heart, open in mind, and infinite in kindness.

Aditi thanked her grandmother a lot as she helped her complete her assignment and made all of them learn many good morals

Lesson from Space:

Wisdom comes from openness and acceptance. Like space holds everything together, we must learn to accept life's vastness, embrace differences, and see the bigger picture.

As they drifted into sleep, their hearts were full—not just with lessons, but with the boundless wisdom of the universe itself.

VIII

The Hidden Treasure of Grandpa's Attic – A Lesson in Gratitude

It was another bright summer morning at Grandma and Grandpa's house. The cousins had already explored the garden, played games, and even visited the fair. But today, there was no real plan, and boredom was creeping in. Even the 5 elements lessons were also finished.

"There's nothing to do!" Alex groaned, lying flat on the wooden floor.

"We've done everything fun already," Shyam sighed.

Just then, Grandpa walked in, carrying his newspaper. "Ah, nothing to do? That reminds me of something exciting!" he said with a twinkle in his eye.

"What? What?" the children sat up eagerly.

Grandpa chuckled. "Have any of you ever been to the attic?"

The cousins exchanged glances. They had never really explored the attic—it was just that old dusty place where Grandma kept things she no longer needed.

"There's an attic?" Srishti's eyes widened.

"Yes, my dears! And I have a feeling there might be a hidden treasure up there," Grandpa said mysteriously.

That was all it took. Within seconds, the children were on their feet, rushing toward the attic stairs.

A Journey into the Past

The attic was dimly lit, with beams of sunlight streaming in through a small window. The air smelled of old books and forgotten memories. Boxes, trunks, and old furniture were stacked all around.

"This place is amazing!" Riddhi exclaimed, running her hands over an old wooden chest.

"Let's start looking for the treasure!" Aditi declared.

The children began opening boxes, each filled with something unexpected—Grandma's old dresses, black-and-white photographs, and even a rusty old telescope.

After some time, Alex, who had been searching in a corner, let out a triumphant yell. "I found something!"

Everyone rushed to see. In his hands was an old, leather-bound diary. The cover was slightly torn, but the golden letters on it read "Memories of My Childhood – By Grandpa."

"You found Grandpa's diary!" Nandini gasped.

"Does this mean... the treasure is a story?" Shyam asked, feeling a little disappointed.

Grandpa, who had climbed up after them, smiled. "Not just a story, my children. This is a treasure more valuable than gold."

The Story of Little Mohan and the Wishing Stone

The cousins sat in a circle as Grandpa opened the diary. "This is a story from my childhood," he said. "A story that taught me the value of gratitude."

The children listened intently as Grandpa began reading.

Many years ago, there was a little boy named Mohan who lived in a small village. Mohan had everything a child could ask for—loving parents, a big mango tree to climb, and friends to play with. But Mohan was never satisfied.

'Why does Raju have a better kite than me?' he would complain. 'Why can't I have new shoes like my cousin?'

One day, while wandering near the river, Mohan found a smooth, glowing stone. A mysterious voice whispered, 'I am the Wishing Stone. You may make one wish, and it shall be granted.'

The children leaned in closer. "What did Mohan wish for, Grandpa?" Srishti asked.

Grandpa continued.

Excited, Mohan wished, 'I want to have everything I desire, instantly!'

The Wishing Stone glowed, and suddenly, Mohan's home was filled with toys, new clothes, and delicious sweets. At first, he was thrilled. But soon, he noticed something strange—no matter what he received, he never felt happy for long. His heart always wanted more.

One day, he met an old man sitting under a banyan tree. The man smiled and asked, 'Tell me, little one, are you happy?'

Mohan hesitated. 'I have everything I ever wanted... but I don't feel happy.'

The old man chuckled. 'Happiness doesn't come from having more. It comes from appreciating what you already have.'

Mohan realized his mistake. He ran back to the river and placed the Wishing Stone in the water. 'I don't want more wishes,' he whispered. 'I just want to be grateful for what I have.' And for the first time in his life, he felt truly happy.

The Real Treasure

Grandpa closed the diary. The attic was silent for a moment. Then Aditi spoke, "So... the real treasure is learning to be grateful?"

Grandpa nodded. "Exactly, my dear. People spend their lives chasing things, thinking that more will make them happy. But true happiness comes from appreciating what you already have."

The children looked around at the attic filled with forgotten treasures—old books, Grandma's handmade shawls, their parents' childhood toys.

"We have so many amazing things right here," Nandini said thoughtfully.

"I guess we don't need a 'real' treasure after all," Alex admitted with a grin.

Grandpa chuckled. "You've already found the greatest treasure of all—the ability to see the value in what you have."

The cousins smiled at one another, feeling lighter and happier. They had come looking for treasure but had found something far more precious—a lesson that would stay with them forever.

Lesson from the Story: Gratitude Brings True Happiness

As the children climbed down from the attic, their hearts were full. That evening, they didn't ask for anything new. Instead, they sat with Grandma and Grandpa, listening to more stories, playing with old toys, and cherishing the simple joys of being together.

And for the first time, they truly understood what it meant to be grateful!

IX

The Great Watermelon Heist – A Lesson in Honesty

The sun was blazing over Grandpa's farm, making the cousins sweaty and restless. They had already played cricket, run around the house twice, and even tried making a lemonade stand (which failed because they drank all the lemonade themselves).

"I'm so hungry," Shyam groaned, flopping onto the porch.

"We just ate lunch," Riddhi reminded him.

"But that was hours ago!"

Aditi wiped her forehead. "I wish we had something juicy and cold to eat."

At that moment, Grandpa walked out, munching on a thick slice of fresh, red watermelon. The juice dripped down his fingers, and his eyes twinkled as he took another bite.

The cousins stared.

"Where did you get that?" Alex asked, practically drooling.

"From the watermelon patch," Grandpa replied, savoring his bite. "But these watermelons are special—only the ripest ones are ready to eat."

Nandini's eyes sparkled. "Let's go pick some for ourselves!"

Grandpa chuckled. "Ah, but only those who are patient get the sweetest ones." He patted his belly and walked inside, leaving the cousins plotting.

The Sneaky Mission Begins

Aditi gathered the group in a huddle. "Okay, new plan. We sneak into the watermelon patch, find the biggest, juiciest one, and enjoy it before Grandpa finds out."

Alex rubbed his hands together. "Operation Watermelon Heist is on!"

They tiptoed toward the field like secret agents, dodging Grandma's watchful eyes as she watered the plants. Finally, they reached the patch—a beautiful stretch of green vines and fat, round watermelons.

Shyam licked his lips. "Look at them... just waiting to be eaten!"

"Shhh," Riddhi whispered. "If Grandpa sees us, we're done for."

The cousins carefully inspected the watermelons. "This one looks huge!" Srishti said, pointing to a massive one in the corner.

Shyam and Alex tried to lift it.

"Ugh, it's so heavy!" Alex grunted.

"Push, don't pull!" Shyam whispered.

As they struggled, they heard a deep voice behind them.

"Trying to steal my watermelons, are you?"

The cousins froze.

They turned around slowly... only to see Grandpa's best

friend, Old Man Ramesh. He was Grandpa's neighbor and the self-proclaimed "Protector of the Watermelon Patch."

Caught Red-Handed!

Old Man Ramesh squinted at them. "Hmmm... sneaking into the patch, eh? What do you have to say for yourselves?"

Aditi cleared her throat. "Uh... we were just... admiring nature?"

"Yes! Studying watermelons for... science!" Srishti added.

Old Man Ramesh raised an eyebrow. "Science, huh? And what do you plan to do with this watermelon?"

The cousins glanced at each other.

"Um... return it?" Alex tried.

But Ramesh grinned. "Aha! Thought so! But I have a deal for you. If you can answer a riddle, I'll let you pick the ripest watermelon myself."

The cousins sighed in relief. A riddle? That was easy!

Ramesh crossed his arms. "Alright, here it is—What can be cracked, made, told, and played?"

The kids exchanged puzzled looks.

"A nut?" Nandini guessed.

"Nope."

"A joke?" Riddhi said hesitantly.

Ramesh beamed. "Correct! A joke! And now, as promised, you get a watermelon—but not just any watermelon."

He led them to a secret corner of the patch where a gigantic watermelon sat. It was almost twice the size of the one they had tried to steal!

"Whoa!" Shyam gasped.

"This is the ripest one here," Ramesh said. "And because you answered honestly, you deserve it."

The Sweetest Watermelon Ever

The cousins rolled the enormous watermelon back home, where Grandpa was already waiting on the porch.

"Well, well," he said, amused. "I see you met Ramesh."

"We tried to steal a watermelon," Alex admitted.

"But then we learned that honesty is sweeter than sneaky plans!" Aditi added.

Grandpa laughed. "That's true. And you know what? The ripest fruits always taste the best when earned the right way."

They cut open the watermelon, and the red, juicy flesh inside made them cheer. As they took big, delicious bites, they agreed—it was the sweetest watermelon they had ever tasted.

And the best part? No sneaky plans were needed.

Lesson from the Story: Honesty Brings the Sweetest Rewards

That night, as they sat on the porch watching fireflies, Grandpa smiled. "See? Sometimes, waiting and doing things the right way makes everything taste better."

The cousins nodded, their bellies full and their hearts even fuller.

And just before bed, Alex muttered, "Next time, let's just ask Grandpa first."

Everyone laughed.

X

The Mystery of the Vanishing Picnic

It was a bright summer morning, and the cousins were feeling restless again. They had spent the last few days playing at Grandpa's house, but today, they wanted something new.

"I'm bored," Shyam groaned, lying flat on the floor like a starfish.

"We need an adventure!" Alex agreed.

At that moment, Grandpa walked in, holding an old, brown picnic basket.

"Ah, I see some grumpy faces here," he chuckled. "Well, I have an idea that might cheer you up—how about a picnic by the lake?"

The room instantly filled with cheers.

"Yes! A picnic!" Aditi clapped her hands.

"Grandma's food tastes even better outdoors!" Srishti added.

Grandpa smiled. "Alright, then. Get ready! But remember—everything must be packed properly, or it might disappear!"

The kids exchanged confused looks. What did that mean? But they were too excited to think about it. They rushed to pack sandwiches, fruit, chips, and of course, Grandma's famous mango pudding.

Once everything was ready, Grandpa loaded up the car, and they set off towards the beautiful lake near the forest.

Little did they know... this would be no ordinary picnic.

The Mysterious Disappearance

After a short drive, they arrived at the perfect spot—a shady tree near the sparkling lake. The cousins ran around excitedly, skipping stones, climbing trees, and chasing butterflies.

Meanwhile, Grandpa and Grandma spread out the picnic blanket and set up the food.

Finally, when everything was ready, Grandma called out, "Come, children! Time to eat!"

The cousins ran back eagerly... only to stop in shock.

"Where's the food?" Nandini gasped.

The picnic basket lay open, but the food inside was gone.

The chips? Gone.

The sandwiches? Gone.

Even the mango pudding? Gone.

Shyam's jaw dropped. "This... this is a disaster!"

"Did a ghost eat our picnic?" Alex whispered dramatically.

Srishti looked around. "Maybe an animal took it?"

Grandpa chuckled. "Ah, so now you see. I told you—things disappear if they're not packed properly!"

"But we did pack them properly!" Riddhi protested.

"Then there's only one explanation," Aditi said, narrowing her eyes. "We have a food thief."

The cousins gasped.

It was time for... The Great Picnic Mystery Investigation.

Operation: Catch the Thief

The cousins split into teams to find clues.

Shyam and Alex inspected the grass near the picnic area. "Look! Breadcrumbs leading towards the bushes!" Alex pointed.

Srishti and Nandini examined footprints near the lake. "These are tiny... not a bear or a dog. Maybe... a raccoon?"

Aditi and Riddhi found something shocking—a trail of mango pudding splatters on the rocks!

They followed the clues carefully, creeping behind bushes and stepping lightly to avoid making noise.

And finally... behind a large tree... they saw the culprits.

A family of monkeys!

There were four of them, happily munching on Grandma's sandwiches while one of them held the mango pudding bowl and licked it clean.

The cousins stared in disbelief.

Shyam whispered, "We got robbed... by monkeys?!"

Alex shook his head. "This is embarrassing."

Just then, one of the monkeys noticed them. It froze—then let out a loud screech!

Within seconds, the entire monkey family scampered up the trees—but not before the smallest monkey accidentally dropped a sandwich right in front of them.

It was the only food left.

"Great," Srishti groaned. "One sandwich. For seven of us."

Grandpa to the Rescue

The cousins trudged back to the picnic spot, disappointed.

Grandma tried to comfort them. "Well, at least we have each other."

Grandpa, however, looked amused.

"Hmm..." he said, stroking his beard. "You kids didn't check my secret compartment, did you?"

"What secret compartment?" Aditi asked, confused.

Grandpa grinned and lifted the bottom layer of the picnic basket.

And there, hidden safely, was another set of sandwiches, fruit, and an extra bowl of mango pudding

"GRANDPA!!" the cousins shouted.

He laughed. "I always pack extra food. I had a feeling those little rascals might show up!"

The cousins cheered as they finally sat down to enjoy their picnic.

The sandwiches tasted even better after the adventure. And as they ate, they couldn't stop laughing about the Great Monkey Picnic Heist.

Moral of the Story: Always Be Prepared!

As they finished their meal, Grandpa leaned back and smiled.

"Life is like a picnic, my dears. Sometimes things go wrong, unexpected problems show up, and monkeys steal your food."

The cousins giggled.

"But if you stay calm, think ahead, and always have a backup plan, you'll still enjoy the journey."

The cousins nodded. Today had started as a disaster... but in the end, it became one of the best picnics ever.

And from that day on, every time they saw a monkey, they laughed and said—

"Better hide the mango pudding!"

XI
The Unexpected Mountain Adventure

The Boring Weekend

It was a hot, lazy afternoon at Grandpa's house. The cousins were lying around, too bored to even play.

"We've done everything already," Shyam complained. "Played games, gone to the park, even caught a thief—"

"A monkey thief," Alex corrected, grinning.

Aditi sighed. "I wish we could go on a real adventure. Something exciting, something big—"

Just then, Grandpa's best friend, Mr. Bhaskar, walked in!

He was a jolly old man with a big belly, a loud laugh, and a habit of wearing colorful hats.

"Hello, hello!" he greeted cheerfully. "I was just passing by and thought I'd invite you all to a very special event!"

The cousins sat up, curious.

"What event?" Srishti asked.

"A fair! But not just any fair," Mr. Bhaskar said dramatically. "This is the Great Mountain Fair of Himtoli! It only happens once a year, and I've arranged a special trip there for tomorrow morning!"

The cousins gasped.

"A trip to the mountains?" Nandini's eyes sparkled.

"An actual out-of-town adventure?" Riddhi added.

"Yes! With rides, games, magic shows, and even a mystery cave!" Mr. Bhaskar wiggled his eyebrows mysteriously.

That was all it took. The cousins begged Grandma and Grandpa to take them.

Grandpa laughed. "Alright, alright! Pack your bags, we leave at dawn!"

And just like that, the great mountain adventure had begun!

The Train Ride Chaos

Early the next morning, the cousins boarded a train to the mountains.

It was their first long train journey together, and they were too excited to sit still!

Alex and Shyam tried to climb the upper berth like monkeys.

Srishti and Nandini bought every snack possible from the train vendors—samosas, peanuts, candy, even a weird-looking pink ice cream.

Aditi and Riddhi got lost trying to find the washroom and ended up in the wrong compartment full of sleeping old uncles!

And at one point, Grandpa fell asleep with his mouth open, snoring so loudly that the entire compartment started laughing!

But the best part?

Just as the train was passing through a dark tunnel, Shyam suddenly screamed—

"AAAH! WHO TOOK MY SANDWICH?!"

The lights flickered back on, and everyone saw Grandpa casually chewing.

"What?" Grandpa said innocently. "I thought it was mine."

The whole compartment burst out laughing.

After hours of fun and chaos, the train finally arrived at the mountain station!

The air was cool and fresh, the mountains looked majestic, and the cousins were ready for adventure!

The Great Mountain Fair

As soon as they reached Himtoli, the cousins ran towards the fairground.

It was magical! Colorful tents, bright lights, and the delicious smell of pakoras, jalebis, and popcorn filled the air.

The fair had everything:

Giant Ferris Wheel – where Alex almost dropped his shoe from the top!

Mirror Maze – where Shyam walked into his own reflection three times.

Magic Show – where Srishti got picked as an assistant and made Grandpa's hat disappear!

Haunted House – where Nandini and Riddhi screamed so loudly that even the fake ghost got scared!

But the biggest attraction of all was...

The Mystery Cave Challenge!

A small sign read:

"Enter the ancient cave and find the hidden treasure! Beware of the tricky paths!"

The cousins couldn't resist.

With Grandpa's permission, they grabbed their flashlights and stepped inside the dark, mysterious cave.

Lost in the Cave!

At first, it was fun. The cave was cool and echoey, and their flashlights flickered against the rocky walls.

"This is so cool!" Aditi whispered.

But then...

BANG!

The entrance slammed shut.

The cousins spun around.

"What just happened?" Srishti gasped.

Shyam gulped. "Uh... I think we're locked in."

The air felt heavy. The cave was silent.

And then... they heard it.

Drip... drip... drip...

A strange sound echoed from the darkness.

"We are officially in a horror movie," Alex muttered.

"No panicking!" Aditi said bravely. "There must be another way out."

The cousins huddled together and walked forward. The cave twisted and turned, leading them deeper inside.

Then suddenly—

"WHO DARES ENTER MY CAVE?"

A deep voice boomed through the darkness.

The cousins froze.

"WHO WAS THAT?!" Nandini whispered in terror.

But just then, their flashlights hit something shiny.

It was a golden box!

They ran towards it and opened it eagerly. Inside, there was...

A note.

It read:

"Congratulations, explorers! You found the treasure of Himtoli Cave! Now follow the glowing arrows to find your way out!"

Just then, small lights flickered along the cave walls, revealing a secret path leading outside.

The cousins cheered!

They had solved the cave challenge!

When they finally stepped out, the fair announcer clapped for them.

"Ladies and gentlemen! These brave children have completed the Mystery Cave Challenge! They win a prize!"

The prize?

A huge basket of sweets and a special adventure badge!

The cousins felt like heroes.

The Ride Back – A Lesson Learned

That evening, as they rode back on the train, Grandpa smiled.

"You see, my little adventurers," he said, "Life is just like today's trip. It's full of surprises, some scary moments, and a few challenges. But if you stick together, think smart, and keep going, you'll always find your way!"

The cousins nodded, munching on their prize sweets.

Shyam sighed happily. "This was the best trip EVER."

And just like that, the great mountain adventure became a story they would never forget.

Moral of the Story: Life is an Adventure!
Be brave in new situations.
Work together to solve problems.
Stay positive even when things get tricky.
And most importantly—always save some snacks for Grandpa

XII

The Crazy Road Trip to the Beach

The Grand Plan

It all started on a hot summer afternoon at Grandpa's house.

The cousins were too restless to sit indoors.

"We need a big trip," Shyam declared. "Something HUGE."

"What about the mountains again?" Nandini suggested.

"No! We already did that," Alex said. "What about—"

"THE BEACH!" Srishti shouted, jumping up.

Everyone gasped.

Yes. The beach.

The cool waves, the golden sand, the ice cream stands—

"YES! We have to go!" Riddhi cheered.

Grandpa and Grandma laughed at their excitement and agreed.

"We'll leave tomorrow morning," Grandpa announced. "Pack your bags, kids! We're going on a road trip!"

Everyone screamed in excitement.

This was going to be the best trip ever!

...Or so they thought.

The Ride Begins... And the Problems Start

The next morning, everyone piled into Grandpa's old, big van.

They packed snacks, sunglasses, beach hats, towels, and even a giant inflatable duck.

"Alright, everyone ready?" Grandpa asked.

"YES!" they all cheered.

Grandpa started the engine.

RRRRR... CLUNK.

The van didn't move.

"Uh-oh," Grandpa said. "Looks like she needs a little push."

So...

ALL the cousins got out and started pushing the van while Grandpa tried again.

After a few minutes of huffing and puffing, the van finally roared to life!

"WE'RE GOING TO THE BEACH!" Aditi shouted.

And off they went.

The Unexpected Detour

For the first hour, the drive was perfect.

The sun was shining, the cousins were singing, and everything was going smoothly.

Until...

BANG!

The van suddenly jerked to a stop.

"What happened?!" Nandini yelped.

Grandpa sighed. "Oh dear. We have a flat tire."

The cousins groaned.

They were stuck in the middle of nowhere, surrounded by trees and not a single shop in sight.

"I knew we should have brought more snacks," Alex muttered.

Just then, they heard a sound.

"MOOOOOO."

Everyone turned.

Behind them stood...

A big brown cow, staring at them like they were trespassers.

"Uh, Grandpa?" Shyam said. "That cow looks... angry."

Before Grandpa could respond, the cow snorted and started walking towards them.

Then it started running.

"RUN!!!" Aditi screamed.

And just like that, the entire family ran in different directions, jumping over bushes, dodging trees, and tripping over roots.

Grandma, however, simply took out a banana from her bag and fed it to the cow.

The cow chewed happily and walked away.

Everyone stared at Grandma.

"...That's it?" Alex panted.

Grandma shrugged. "Sometimes, all a problem needs is a snack."

Back on the Road... Or Not

After Grandpa fixed the tire, they continued driving.

"We're back on track!" Riddhi cheered.

But just 10 minutes later…

"Uh, Grandpa?" Srishti said. "Why is there water on the road?"

Grandpa slowed down.

Ahead of them was a huge flooded road.

"We can't go through that!" Aditi gasped.

"We have to find another way," Grandpa said.

So… they turned onto a small side road.

At first, it was fine.

Then it got narrower.

Then bumpier.

Then suddenly—

BUMP!

The van dipped into a HUGE pothole and stopped.

"We're stuck," Grandpa sighed.

The cousins groaned loudly.

"WE WILL NEVER REACH THE BEACH!" Shyam wailed.

"This is the worst trip ever!" Alex cried.

But then…

Grandpa smiled.

"You kids wanted an adventure, right?" he said.

They all stared at him.

"Well… yeah," Aditi admitted.

"Then let's turn this into an adventure," Grandpa said. "Instead of getting upset, let's fix the problem together."

The cousins exchanged glances.

Then—

"Let's do it!" Riddhi grinned.

The Rescue Mission

Everyone worked together to get the van out of the pothole.

Aditi and Nandini found big rocks to place under the tires.

Alex and Shyam pushed from behind.

Srishti and Riddhi cheered loudly.

And finally...

VROOM!

The van rolled out of the pothole!

"YES!" The cousins jumped and cheered.

Grandpa patted their heads. "See? Teamwork wins every time."

FINALLY... THE BEACH!

After hours of chaos, the cousins finally saw the ocean.

The moment Grandpa parked, they all jumped out, screaming in joy.

They splashed in the water, built giant sandcastles, and ate ice creams bigger than their faces.

Grandpa and Grandma relaxed under an umbrella, watching them with a smile.

That evening, as the sun set, the cousins sat together, watching the waves.

"You know," Shyam said, "this trip didn't go as planned..."

"...But it was the most fun we've ever had!" Alex finished.

Grandpa chuckled. "That's life for you. The best adventures come from the unexpected."

The cousins smiled.

They had set out for a simple beach trip.

But they got a wild road trip, a cow chase, a teamwork challenge, and memories they would never forget.

And as they ran back into the waves one last time, they all agreed—

This was the best trip ever.

Moral of the Story: Every Problem is an Adventure!

Sometimes, things don't go as planned—but that doesn't mean they aren't fun!

Teamwork and a good attitude can turn any problem into an adventure.

And most importantly... never underestimate a cow!

XIII

Day 1: The Great Train Adventure with Doughnut

It was the most exciting day of summer vacation—the cousins, along with Grandma, Grandpa, and their parents, were going on a train journey to a beautiful hill station! The entire house was buzzing with excitement as bags were packed, last-minute snacks were stuffed into handbags, and everyone ran around making sure nothing was forgotten.

But the most excited of all? Doughnut, their adorable pet rabbit!

Doughnut was fluffy, round, and white as a soft cloud. He had the cutest twitching nose and the habit of hopping into anyone's lap whenever they sat down. All the cousins absolutely adored him—especially Srishti and Nandini, who treated him like a baby.

As they reached the railway station, the adventure truly began. The platform was crowded with travelers, vendors calling out, "Chai! Samosa! Cold drinks!" and coolies rushing by with heavy suitcases.

Doughnut sat snugly in his little carrier, his tiny pink nose twitching in excitement. He peeked through the small opening, watching the chaos of the platform.

"Do you think he knows we're going on a trip?" Aditi giggled.

"Of course! He's a smart rabbit," Shyam said proudly.

Finally, the train whooshed into the station, its whistle blowing loudly. The cousins jumped in excitement as Grandpa called out, "All aboard! Let's go, let's go!"

They climbed onto the train and found their seats in a cozy compartment. The cousins had a window seat, and as soon as the train started moving, they pressed their faces against the glass, watching the scenery blur past.

Doughnut's Train Mischief

As the train rolled on, the cousins opened their snack bags and began munching. They had brought Grandma's special laddoos, samosas, chips, and mango juice.

Meanwhile, Doughnut sat in his carrier, looking longingly at the food.

"Aww, poor thing must be hungry," Riddhi said, opening the carrier door slightly.

And that's when it happened.

WHOOSH!

Doughnut leaped out like a fluffy rocket and landed straight on Grandpa's lap!

"AHH! What in the world—" Grandpa yelped as Doughnut sniffed his pocket curiously.

The cousins burst into laughter.

"He thinks you're hiding a treat, Grandpa!" Nandini giggled.

Grandpa sighed, shaking his head. "This little fellow is too smart."

Doughnut, however, had no interest in sitting quietly. He hopped onto the top bunk, startling Alex, who almost spilled his juice. Then, he jumped onto Aditi's shoulder, making her squeal with laughter.

"He's turning the train into his playground!" Shyam laughed.

After some effort, they finally got Doughnut back into his carrier—but not before he stole a tiny bite of Grandma's laddoo.

"Hey! That's mine!" Srishti cried, but Doughnut just twitched his nose innocently.

Reaching the Hill Station

After hours of fun, naps, and games, the train finally pulled into the hill station. A cool breeze welcomed them as they stepped onto the platform.

They took a jeep ride up the hills to their hotel, which was a beautiful wooden lodge surrounded by tall pine trees. The air smelled fresh, and the sound of birds chirping filled the air.

Their hotel room was huge, with soft beds, a cozy fireplace, and a balcony that overlooked the mountains.

"This place is AMAZING!" Alex shouted, jumping onto the bed.

Grandma shook her head. "No jumping! The beds are for sleeping, not bouncing."

Doughnut, on the other hand, was already exploring. He hopped onto the soft carpet, sniffing everything.

"What if he gets lost?" Aditi worried.

"No way," Shyam said. "He's the boss of this trip."

Just then, Doughnut hopped onto the balcony, and everyone ran after him.

"Doughnut, no!" Srishti gasped.

But the rabbit just sat there peacefully, staring at the sunset.

The cousins joined him, sitting together as they watched the sky turn golden-orange.

"This is the best trip ever," Riddhi whispered.

And with their fluffy companion by their side, it truly felt like a perfect start to their adventure.

Next up: Day 2 - Exploring the Hill Station! Will Doughnut behave? Or will he create more mischief?

Let's see!!!

XIV

Day 2: Doughnut, the Hill Station Explorer!

The next morning, the cousins woke up to the chirping of birds and the fresh mountain breeze. The hotel's wooden floors creaked softly as they ran around, getting ready for the day's adventure.

But the happiest of all? Doughnut! The fluffy little rabbit was already hopping around, sniffing the air excitedly.

"Looks like Doughnut is ready for adventure!" Aditi laughed, watching him bounce around like a cotton ball.

Grandpa stretched and yawned. "Alright, kids! Today, we're going to explore the famous hill station market, take a nature walk, and have a picnic by the lake. And of course, Doughnut will come along!"

"YAYYY!" the cousins cheered.

A Fluffy Star in the Market

The hill station market was bustling with activity—shops lined both sides of the street, selling colorful woolen sweaters, handcrafted toys, and delicious snacks like hot jalebis, roasted corn, and steaming momos.

The moment Doughnut hopped out of his carrier, the entire market went wild!

"Oh my goodness! Look at that adorable rabbit!" a shopkeeper's daughter squealed.

People gathered around, staring at Doughnut like he was a celebrity.

A group of elderly tourists even asked, "Can we take a picture with him?"

Doughnut sat majestically on Shyam's shoulder, twitching his nose like a royal prince.

Aditi smirked. "Looks like Doughnut is more famous than any of us!"

The cousins couldn't stop laughing as they moved through the market, with Doughnut getting more attention than the hill station itself.

The "Great Corn Chase"

While walking past a street vendor, Doughnut's nose twitched rapidly.

"Oh no," Nandini whispered. "I know that face."

Before anyone could react, Doughnut leaped off Aditi's arm, straight towards a pile of fresh, hot roasted corn!

"DOUGHNUT, NOOOO!" the cousins screamed, running after him.

The vendor, a burly man with a thick mustache, gasped. "Heyyy! Catch that bunny! He's stealing my corn!"

Doughnut, however, grabbed a piece of corn in his tiny mouth and took off down the street like a furry rocket!

The cousins, the shopkeeper, and even some random tourists chased after him, dodging bicycles, jumping over crates, and startling a poor dog who yelped in confusion.

After five minutes of complete chaos, Doughnut finally stopped—right in front of a little boy who was crying because he had dropped his corn.

Everyone watched in surprise as Doughnut gently placed the corn in the boy's hands.

The boy's face lit up with joy. "Thank you, bunny!"

The vendor, who had been panting from the chase, burst out laughing. "Well, I can't be mad at that! That's one special rabbit!"

The cousins sighed in relief, picking up Doughnut.

"Remind me never to let him near food again," Alex groaned.

But the adventure wasn't over yet!

Picnic by the Lake & The Mystery of the Missing Sandwich

After all the excitement, they finally reached a beautiful lake surrounded by tall pine trees. The water was so clear that they could see tiny fish swimming beneath the surface.

They spread out their picnic blanket and opened their baskets—sandwiches, fresh fruit, juice, and Grandma's homemade cookies.

Doughnut sat peacefully on Riddhi's lap, watching the lake with his little ears twitching.

"This is so peaceful," Aditi sighed happily.

Until...

"HEY! Where's my sandwich?!" Shyam shouted.

Everyone turned to see his plate was empty.

"What?! But it was right there!" Nandini gasped.

Then they saw it. A tiny white fluffy tail disappearing into the bushes.

"DOUGHNUT!!" they all shouted.

The mischievous rabbit had snuck away with Shyam's sandwich!

They ran after him (again!), only to find Doughnut happily munching on the sandwich, looking completely innocent.

Shyam groaned. "I can't believe this. I got outsmarted by a rabbit."

The cousins burst into laughter.

Grandpa shook his head, wiping away tears of laughter. "Doughnut, you little rascal! You've given us the funniest trip ever!"

XV

Day 3: The Most Unforgettable Day!

The last morning at the hotel arrived way too soon. The golden sun peeked through the curtains, and the cousins stretched lazily, realizing this was their final full day of fun before heading home.

But there was no time to be sad—this day had to be the most exciting, the most hilarious, and the most memorable!

As usual, Doughnut was up first. He hopped onto Aditi's bed and started nibbling on her blanket.

"Ahhh! Doughnut, that's my blanket, not breakfast!" Aditi laughed, pulling it away.

Everyone woke up one by one, yawning, stretching, and realizing—TODAY HAD TO BE EPIC.

The Great Breakfast Fiasco!

The first order of business? The Grand Hotel Breakfast Buffet.

The cousins ran down to the dining hall, where tables were filled with the most delicious food—hot pancakes, crispy dosas, fluffy omelets, fresh fruits, and steaming cups of hot chocolate!

"We have to try EVERYTHING!" Alex announced.

And they did. Plates were stacked high, and laughter filled the air.

But then—the Great Mishap happened.

As Shyam reached for the honey jar, Doughnut suddenly decided it was a great time to hop onto the table.

The jar wobbled... and...

SPLAT! Honey spilled everywhere!

Right on Grandpa's plate.

The cousins froze.

Grandpa looked at his honey-covered dosa and then at Doughnut, who was licking honey off his tiny paws, looking completely innocent.

For a moment, silence.

Then—Grandpa burst into laughter!

"Well, I always wanted extra honey on my dosa, but this might be a little too much!" he chuckled.

The entire table erupted in laughter. Even the hotel staff smiled as they helped clean up.

A Surprise from the Hotel!

After breakfast, as they were about to head out, the hotel manager approached them.

"You kids have been our happiest guests!" he said with a smile. "As a special farewell gift, we have arranged a fun treasure hunt inside the hotel!"

"A TREASURE HUNT?!" the cousins cheered.

Doughnut wiggled his nose excitedly. Even he wanted in on the fun.

Each cousin got a clue card, leading them to different places—the swimming pool, the garden, the rooftop café, and even the laundry room (where Alex almost got stuck in a pile of fresh towels).

Finally, they reached the hotel's big lounge, where a small wooden treasure box was waiting.

Inside?

Personalized keychains for each of them—with their names and a tiny golden bunny charm for Doughnut!

"This is the BEST hotel ever!" Srishti said, hugging her keychain.

The Most Epic Pillow Fight!

After returning to their room, nobody wanted the day to end.

"We have to do something crazy before we leave," Riddhi declared.

A moment of silence.

Then...

Shyam grabbed a pillow.

Aditi grabbed another.

"PILLOW FIGHT!!!!"

And chaos began.

Feathers flew. Pillows soared. Laughter echoed. Doughnut hopped around, dodging flying pillows like a tiny ninja.

Just as Alex was about to launch a mega pillow attack, the door opened—

And in walked Grandma.

The cousins froze mid-battle.

Pillows hung in the air. Feathers drifted to the ground.

Grandma narrowed her eyes at the mess...

And then—

She grabbed a pillow and SMACK! Right on Shyam's head!

"GRANDMA'S IN THE GAME!" Riddhi screamed.

The fight resumed with double energy.

It was the most legendary pillow fight in family history.

A Sunset to Remember

Finally, exhausted, everyone flopped onto the bed, panting, laughing, and covered in feathers.

As the sun began to set, they went to the hotel rooftop to watch their final evening together.

The sky was painted in hues of orange and pink, the distant mountains glowing in the golden light.

"This was the best trip ever," Nandini sighed happily.

"And the best hotel," Aditi added.

"And the best adventure," Alex grinned.

"And the best pillow fight!" Shyam laughed.

They all turned to Doughnut, who sat comfortably in Riddhi's lap, licking his tiny paws, looking completely satisfied with himself.

"And of course," Grandma smiled, "the best little travel buddy in the world."

Doughnut twitched his ears and gave a tiny happy hop.

Tomorrow, they would go home.

But tonight?

Tonight was for laughter, for memories, and for the joy of simply being together.

To Be Continued...

Or maybe... the journey home will have its surprises!

XVI

Day 4: The Journey Home – But Not Without Surprises!

The morning sun streamed through the curtains as the cousins slowly stirred awake, realizing this was it—the day they had to leave the hotel and head home.

There was a mixture of sadness and excitement.

Sadness because the trip had been so much fun.

Excitement because... well, knowing this family, anything could happen on the way home.

The Last Hotel Breakfast (And Doughnut's Secret Plan)

Downstairs, the final hotel breakfast was waiting. The cousins decided to eat extra slowly—stretching the meal as long as possible.

Doughnut, however, had other plans.

The little rabbit had gotten quite comfortable at the hotel, and it seemed he wasn't ready to leave just yet.

As everyone packed their bags, Doughnut vanished.

"Where is he?!" Aditi panicked, looking under the bed.

"Maybe he's in the suitcase again?" Nandini suggested.

"Not this time," Alex said, holding up his bag, which was suspiciously lighter than usual.

Then, Grandpa started laughing.

Everyone turned.

There was Doughnut—sitting on a hotel cart, looking like a VIP guest, being rolled away by a friendly hotel staff member.

"I think he wants to stay," the man chuckled.

"Doughnut, you little rascal!" Riddhi scooped him up.

Doughnut wiggled his nose mischievously as if saying, Well, it was worth a try.

The Train Ride – Chaos Begins!

Finally, they reached the train station. The cousins loved train rides—peering out the window, buying snacks from vendors, and playing endless games.

But first... the challenge of getting Doughnut settled.

They had bought a special small travel basket for him, but Doughnut, being Doughnut, had other ideas.

Just as they got onto the train, he wiggled out of the basket and hopped straight onto an empty seat.

An old lady sitting nearby gasped. "Oh my! What a cute little thing!"

Instead of causing trouble, Doughnut had won her heart instantly.

"Such a polite rabbit," she said, stroking his soft fur. "Unlike my grandson—he never listens!"

The cousins giggled. Doughnut had made yet another fan.

Snack Time Disaster!

Train rides meant one important thing—snacks!

Grandma had packed parathas, laddoos, chips, and juice boxes. The cousins dug in happily.

But then...

Shyam opened a packet of spicy chips and left it unattended for just a second.

Doughnut saw his chance.

He nibbled a tiny piece before anyone could stop him.

For a second, everything was normal.

Then—Doughnut's nose twitched.

His little ears perked up.

And then—

ACHOO!

A tiny rabbit sneeze echoed through the train compartment.

Then another. And another.

The cousins burst into laughter.

Doughnut shook his fluffy head, sneezed one last time, and gave Shyam an angry look.

How dare you let me eat spicy chips!

"I think Doughnut's telling you never to leave food unattended again," Riddhi giggled.

Shyam scratched his head. "Noted."

The Unexpected Train Stop!

Just as they were all settling in, the train suddenly jerked to a halt.

A voice on the speaker crackled:

"Passengers, due to a small delay, the train will stop here for 30 minutes."

The cousins looked out the window—they had stopped at a small countryside station.

And right outside?

A tiny market with food stalls, toys, and souvenirs!

"Should we go explore?" Aditi asked excitedly.

Grandpa checked the time. "We have 30 minutes—let's make it quick!"

Mini Adventure at the Station Market!

The cousins rushed out, eager to see what the tiny station market had to offer.

There were:

✓ Clay toys that looked hand-painted.

✓ Fruity kulfi in earthen pots.

✓ A man selling balloons shaped like animals!

The balloon seller smiled at Doughnut. "For your bunny, I have just the thing!"

He handed them a tiny pink rabbit-shaped balloon.

Doughnut sniffed it curiously and then bounced happily.

"Looks like he approves!" Nandini laughed. Just as they were about to leave, the cousins spotted a small puppet show happening under a banyan tree.

The puppeteer was telling a funny story about a mischievous monkey stealing a traveler's hat.

It was so hilarious that the cousins couldn't stop laughing. Even Grandma and Grandpa chuckled.

It was the perfect way to spend their unexpected break.

Back on the Train—Heading Home!

Soon, the train whistle blew, and they rushed back aboard.

Everyone settled into their seats, exhausted but happy.

Doughnut curled up in Riddhi's lap, hugging his pink balloon.

The cousins chatted about their favorite moments from the trip—from the hotel fun to the pillow fight, the treasure hunt, and now this surprise stop!

"It was the best trip ever," Aditi sighed happily.

Grandma smiled. "Every journey is special. But the best part is—every journey brings a new adventure. And you never know what's coming next!"

Doughnut wiggled his nose in agreement.

As the train chugged along, the cousins drifted off to sleep, dreaming of the next adventure waiting for them... somewhere, someday.

Because with this family, there was always another adventure just around the corner!

The End (Or Maybe... The Beginning of Another Adventure?)

XVII

Day 5: Homecoming & The Great Birthday Surprise Mission Begins!

As the train slowed down and the platform came into view, the cousins stirred from their naps. Shyam stretched so hard that he almost smacked Alex in the face.

"Watch it, man!" Alex grumbled, dodging just in time.

Aditi, still half-asleep, yawned. "Are we there yet?"

"YES! FINALLY!" Srishti cheered, bouncing on her seat. "I missed my bed!"

"You missed your bed?" Nandini smirked. "I missed my mom's food!"

As the train came to a halt, excitement buzzed through the

air. They grabbed their bags, making sure Doughnut was safely tucked in his travel carrier. The fluffy rabbit twitched his nose, unaware of the chaos about to unfold.

The moment they stepped onto the platform, their mothers rushed toward them with big smiles.

"Oh, look at my babies!" Aditi's mother gushed, hugging her tightly.

"Why do you all look so... messy?" Nandini's mom raised an eyebrow. "What kind of adventure have you been on?"

The kids exchanged guilty looks. Between Doughnut's antics, the hotel chaos, and the train ride, their vacation had been eventful, to say the least.

"Nothing much," Shyam said innocently. "Just, you know, the usual."

The mothers shook their heads and led them toward the car. But unknown to Aditi, a secret plan was already in motion.

Mission: The Ultimate Birthday Surprise!

As soon as they got home, Aditi sighed happily. "I'm going straight to my bed!" she announced, dropping her bag dramatically.

"Yes, yes, you must rest!" Shyam said, exchanging a look with the others.

"Get all the sleep you need," Riddhi added, a little too cheerfully.

Aditi narrowed her eyes. "Why are you guys acting so weird?"

"Weird? Us? Never!" Alex said, pushing her toward her room. Aditi, too tired to argue, shrugged and disappeared into her room. The moment her door shut, the real fun began.

"Okay, listen up!" Shyam whispered as the cousins huddled in the living room. "We have less than a day to make this the best birthday ever!"

"We need decorations, a cake, and the best distraction plan," Srishti added.

"And someone needs to keep Aditi far away from the living room," Nandini said.

Alex grinned. "Leave that to me."

Step 1: Operation Distraction

The next morning, as soon as Aditi woke up, Alex burst into her room.

"Aditi! You have to come outside right now!" he shouted.

"Why? What happened?" Aditi rubbed her eyes.

"It's Doughnut!" Alex said dramatically. "I think he's... he's...." He paused for effect.

Aditi gasped. "WHAT HAPPENED TO DOUGHNUT?!"

"He's doing something really weird!" Alex said, leading her away from the house.

Outside, the other cousins were waiting with Doughnut, who was completely fine.

"See? He's acting strange!" Alex said, pointing at the rabbit, who was just... nibbling on a leaf.

Aditi frowned. "That's normal, Alex."

"No, no, look closer!" Shyam insisted. "I swear he just did a backflip!"

"A backflip?!" Aditi leaned in, staring intensely at Doughnut. The rabbit blinked.

The cousins exchanged amused glances.

"Maybe we should wait a little longer," Nandini suggested, trying not to laugh.

Aditi sighed. "I guess I can stay out a bit more."

Step 2: The Party Prep Frenzy

Back in the house, the mothers were busy in the kitchen, making a grand feast. Meanwhile, the cousins transformed the living room into a magical party zone.

Shyam and Alex blew up balloons—except Alex kept

popping them accidentally.

"STOP IT!" Shyam groaned as another balloon exploded.

"It's not my fault!" Alex protested. "These things are evil!"

Meanwhile, Srishti and Riddhi were decorating a giant cake with chocolate frosting and extra sprinkles.

"We should make it extra special," Riddhi said.

Srishti grinned. "How about we write 'Happy Birthday, Aditi' in rainbow-colored icing?"

"Perfect!"

On the other side of the room, Nandini was setting up a special surprise—Doughnut's outfit!

"He's gonna wear a little bowtie!" she squealed, holding up a tiny pink bow.

Grandpa walked in and chuckled. "That poor rabbit. He has no idea what's coming."

Step 3: Keeping Aditi Out of the House

Back outside, Aditi was still watching Doughnut, waiting for the so-called backflip.

"Maybe I should just go inside—" she started.

"WAIT!" Alex blurted out. "Uhh... we should take Doughnut for a walk!"

"In this heat?" Aditi raised an eyebrow.

"Uh... YES!" Shyam jumped in. "Doughnut loves walks!"

Aditi squinted at them. "Since when?"

The cousins exchanged nervous glances.

"Since... today?" Alex said.

Before Aditi could ask more questions, Riddhi ran out. "OH NO! The mangoes in the backyard are falling! We need help picking them!"

"Mangoes?" Aditi looked confused.

"YES! And they're rolling everywhere!"

And so, for the next hour, Aditi was kept busy running after completely normal mangoes, while inside, the final decorations were set.

The Grand Surprise!

Finally, everything was ready. The living room was sparkling with fairy lights, colorful balloons, and a giant "Happy Birthday, Aditi!" banner. Doughnut sat proudly in his bowtie, looking like the true star of the show.

When Aditi finally walked in, everyone shouted—

"SURPRISE!!!"

Aditi gasped. "Wha—what?! YOU GUYS PLANNED THIS?!" She looked around in awe. The cake, the decorations, the effort—she was completely overwhelmed.

"You... you did all this for me?"

"Of course!" Shyam grinned.

"You're our favorite cousin!" Riddhi added.

Aditi's Birthday Surprise Continues!

Aditi blinked, still taking in the decorations, the twinkling fairy lights, and the grand chocolate cake sitting at the center of the room.

"You guys..." she started, her voice filled with emotion.

"Don't get all teary on us!" Alex teased, nudging her. "We still have the best part left—the cake!"

Doughnut, still wearing his tiny bowtie, twitched his nose and hopped excitedly toward Aditi, as if agreeing. The girls immediately scooped him up, showering him with affection.

"Oh my gosh, look at him! He looks like a little prince!" Nandini squealed.

Aditi laughed and held him close. "This is seriously the best birthday ever!"

"Well, it's not over yet!" Shyam announced. "Time to cut the cake!"

Everyone gathered around as Aditi made a wish and blew out the candles.

"Alright, first bite goes to—" Aditi paused dramatically.

"Doughnut!" Srishti declared, before anyone could argue.

"You can't give chocolate to a rabbit!" Riddhi giggled.

"Fine, fine!" Aditi laughed. "Then... the first bite goes to Grandma!"

Grandma, who had been watching the whole scene with a warm smile, stepped forward. "Oh, my dear, this is the sweetest gesture. But the real sweetness is seeing you all work together and make this day so special."

Aditi grinned and fed her the first piece. Soon, everyone was digging into the delicious cake, laughing and enjoying the moment.

Let the Fun Begin!

Just as everyone was finishing their slices, Alex stood up. "Okay, time for party games!"

"What kind of games?" Srishti asked, raising an eyebrow.

"The best kind," Shyam smirked. "The ones where we make fools of ourselves!"

The first game was "Balloon Pop Challenge," where everyone had to sit on a balloon until it popped.

Shyam went first. He dramatically jumped onto his balloon, but instead of popping, it slipped out from under him and shot across the room like a rocket.

Everyone burst out laughing as he landed flat on his back.

"FAIL!" Alex shouted, clapping.

"You try it then, genius!" Shyam grumbled.

Alex confidently sat on his balloon, but instead of popping, it made an embarrassing squeaky noise.

The room exploded into laughter again.

"Okay, okay! Let's move to the next game," Aditi said between giggles.

The next was "Pin the Bowtie on Doughnut"—except Doughnut, being a rabbit, refused to sit still. Every time someone got close, he would hop away, making everyone chase him around the living room.

"Hold still, Doughnut!" Riddhi cried, breathless from running.

But Doughnut, enjoying the attention, zoomed around like a tiny fluffy tornado.

The laughter didn't stop as they moved from game to game, from charades to a hilarious round of musical chairs where Grandma surprisingly won!

The Final Surprise

Just when Aditi thought the party couldn't get any better, her mother stepped forward.

"Aditi, we have one more surprise for you."

Aditi's eyes widened. "Another one?! What is it?"

Her mother handed her a small, wrapped box. Aditi quickly tore it open and gasped.

Inside was a beautifully framed photo of all the cousins, taken during their vacation. But that wasn't all—it had a little engraving at the bottom:

"Best Moments Are Spent Together."

Aditi's heart swelled. She looked around at her family, at Doughnut happily nibbling on a piece of fruit, at the decorations, and at the smiling faces of the people she loved the most.

"This... is the best gift ever," she whispered.

"Happy Birthday, Aditi!" everyone cheered.

And with that, the party continued late into the night, filled with love, laughter, and memories they would never forget.

Birthday Decorations With Doughnut

XVIII

The Day After Aditi's Surprise Birthday Party

The morning after Aditi's birthday was a calm, peaceful one. After all the excitement from the night before, everyone was still in the cozy glow of the surprise party. Doughnut, of course, had slept like a king, tucked into his little bunny bed, not a care in the world.

Aditi woke up early, still feeling the warmth from yesterday's celebrations. She smiled to herself as she walked into the living room, where her cousins were already gathered.

"Good morning, birthday girl!" Shyam grinned, handing her a cup of hot chocolate.

"Thanks!" Aditi smiled, accepting the cup. She had to admit, she was a little sad that all the birthday excitement had come to an end.

"Feeling like a queen?" Nandini asked, plopping down next

to her. "You should! You were the star of the show!"

"Yeah, but now that it's over, it feels kind of... empty, doesn't it?" Aditi sighed, taking a sip of her drink. "No more surprises, no more games."

"We've got a solution for that!" Alex said, winking. "We're going on a post-birthday adventure!"

Everyone looked at him, eyebrows raised.

"You've been planning this?!" Aditi exclaimed, almost spilling her hot chocolate in shock.

"Yup!" Shyam chimed in. "After all the birthday fun, we thought you could use one more surprise. Plus, we've got Doughnut to keep us company!"

Aditi felt her excitement bubble up again. "Wait, wait! What are we doing? Where are we going?"

"You'll see," Riddhi teased, "But trust me, you're gonna love it. It's going to be just as fun as yesterday."

The Secret Adventure

The cousins packed up their things in a flash, and Aditi couldn't help but feel a little giddy. Even Doughnut, in his tiny travel carrier, seemed to sense something exciting was coming up, as he hopped around enthusiastically.

After a quick breakfast, everyone piled into Grandpa's big white car, including Doughnut, who had his own little plush seat right between the cousins.

"Where are we going?!" Aditi asked over and over again as they drove through the city. She tried peeking out the windows to catch a glimpse of any signs, but all she saw were familiar streets.

"You'll know when we get there!" Alex said with a grin.

As they passed through the outskirts of town, Aditi's curiosity was nearly unbearable. "Are we going to a theme park?" she guessed, her eyes lighting up.

"Not quite," Shyam said. "But you'll see, it's going to be

something just as amazing."

They drove for what felt like an eternity before finally pulling into a quiet, charming area with tall trees and colorful flowers. A huge sign at the entrance read, "Sunny Meadows Farm and Petting Zoo."

Aditi's eyes went wide. "This is the surprise?" she gasped, practically jumping out of the car.

"Yep!" Riddhi smiled. "We thought you'd enjoy a day at the farm! And look—there's a petting zoo!"

The cousins, along with Doughnut, excitedly made their way toward the entrance. The farm was alive with sounds—chirping birds, bleating goats, and the rustle of animals in their pens.

A Day at the Farm

The first stop was the petting zoo, where Aditi and the others could interact with cute, friendly animals. They immediately ran to the goats, which were happily munching on hay. Doughnut, sensing the other animals, twitched his nose and hopped out of his carrier, eager to explore the new environment.

"Look at him go!" Srishti laughed as Doughnut bounded around the goats. One particularly curious goat took a liking to Doughnut, sniffing him gently. "Looks like he's making a new friend!"

The next stop was the bunny pen. Aditi gasped as she saw dozens of fluffy rabbits hopping around. "I think I found my spirit animal!" she joked, falling in love with every single rabbit.

"Alright, alright," Shyam said, laughing, "Let's not forget about the llamas!"

They walked over to the llama pen, where the long-necked creatures were lazily munching grass. "They're so cute!" Nandini exclaimed. "But do they spit?"

"Only when they're in a bad mood," Alex warned, eyeing one of the llamas suspiciously.

Soon, everyone was rolling with laughter as the llamas strutted about, trying to steal food from the goats. But the real surprise came when they saw a baby alpaca, which was the softest thing they had ever touched.

Doughnut, not to be left behind, had a grand time hopping around the pen, chasing after the baby alpaca. "You know," Shyam said, "Doughnut could start his own petting zoo at this rate."

After a couple of hours of playing and laughing with the animals, the group made their way to the picnic area. They sat under a large tree, enjoying sandwiches and snacks that Grandma had packed.

"This is so perfect," Aditi said between bites of her sandwich. "It's the best way to end the birthday surprises!"

"We told you, there's always something exciting happening with us," Alex said with a wink.

"I don't know how you guys do it," Aditi said with a grin. "But I've never had a more fun day in my life."

As the sun began to set and the day came to a close, the cousins piled back into the car, their hearts full of happiness and laughter. Doughnut, exhausted from his adventure, nestled into Aditi's lap, looking as content as ever.

It had been a perfect day—a day full of animals, laughter, and memories that would last forever. As they drove back home, Aditi couldn't help but think that this trip was the best birthday surprise yet.

"Thanks, guys," Aditi said, looking at each of her cousins with a warm smile. "This was the best birthday I've ever had. Not just the party, but everything. Thank you for making it so special."

"You're welcome, birthday girl!" Shyam said, reaching over to mess with her hair.

"And just remember," Riddhi added, "the best part of any surprise is the people you share it with."

The car hummed along the road, and Doughnut let out a contented little snore as the cousins shared one last round of giggles, knowing this was a day they would never forget.

XIX

The Last Day of Vacation - A Day to Remember

The sun shone brightly through the windows of Grandma and Grandpa's house, signaling that today was the final day of the cousins' vacation. After the whirlwind of Aditi's birthday celebration the day before, the house was filled with laughter and excitement—yet a bittersweet feeling lingered in the air. Tomorrow, they would all have to return to their homes. But today... Today was about making the most of every moment they had left together.

The cousins gathered in the living room, sipping their juice and nibbling on some of Grandma's homemade snacks. Doughnut, their adorable, fluffy pet rabbit, was nestled in Aditi's lap, looking as content as ever. He had become an integral part of their vacation, and the cousins couldn't imagine returning home without him.

Grandpa, who had been quietly observing the cousins, stood up with a twinkle in his eye. "I know you all are getting ready to leave, but before you go, I have something for each of you."

The cousins looked at each other, curious. "What is it, Grandpa?" Shyam asked, his eyes wide with anticipation.

Grandpa smiled and reached into a small drawer, pulling out a box wrapped in bright paper. "It's a little something to remember this vacation by."

He handed a box to each cousin, and their faces lit up as they tore off the wrapping. Inside were personalized gifts:

Aditi received a delicate necklace with a charm shaped like a rabbit, reminding her of Doughnut and the fun moments they had together.

Shyam got a mini compass, symbolizing the adventures they had and all the places they'd explore in the future.

Riddhi found a small sketchbook, with a set of colorful pens—her passion for drawing had flourished during the trip, and Grandpa knew she'd love to capture their memories.

Nandini opened a beautiful framed photo of the cousins with Doughnut, taken on their first day at Grandma and Grandpa's house.

Srishti was gifted a handcrafted wooden puzzle, a token of all the games they had played together.

Alex found a pair of binoculars, perfect for his curiosity and love of exploring.

"This is so thoughtful!" Aditi exclaimed, hugging Grandpa. "Thank you so much!"

Grandma, who had been quietly watching, smiled and walked over to them. "And I have something for all of you as well," she said, her voice warm.

She handed each cousin a small journal, with a soft, leather cover and a gold-embossed design. "These journals are for you to write down your memories from this trip. It's always nice to remember the fun times, but it's even better to have a place to keep them close to your heart."

The cousins, touched by Grandma's words, each took a journal and thanked her. "We'll write in them every day!" Nandini promised.

As the day unfolded, they spent their time enjoying the little moments. They had one last walk around the garden, where Grandma showed them her favorite flowers and explained how she had nurtured them over the years. Grandpa played his usual tricks, pretending to fall asleep and then suddenly scaring the cousins with his loud "BOO!"—making everyone laugh until they were in stitches.

Doughnut, as always, was the center of attention. He hopped around playfully, snuggling into their laps whenever he could. "I'm going to miss him so much," Srishti said, her voice full of affection as she scratched behind his ears. "He's the best travel buddy!"

That evening, as the sun began to set and the sky turned into hues of orange and pink, Grandma prepared a special dinner for the family. Everyone sat around the table, savoring the delicious food and chatting about their favorite memories.

"Remember the time we tried to make the sandcastle at the beach?" Alex laughed. "It looked like a pile of sand at first, but then we finally got it right!"

"And how about the train journey?" Riddhi added. "Doughnut was a superstar, sitting on everyone's laps!"

"I'll never forget that little picnic we had in the park," Aditi said. "It felt so peaceful just sitting there, enjoying the simple things."

Grandpa raised his glass, signaling a toast. "Here's to family, adventures, and memories that will last forever," he said with a grin.

The cousins clinked their glasses together, feeling grateful for the time they had spent together.

After dinner, Grandma and Grandpa surprised them with one final gift—a box of chocolate chip cookies. "These are for the road," Grandma said, winking. "Take them with you and think of us whenever you nibble on one."

As the evening drew to a close, the cousins sat together, their hearts full of happiness and gratitude. They'd made so many memories during this vacation, and even though tomorrow meant returning to their separate homes, they knew they would always be connected by the love and laughter they shared.

"Let's promise to meet again soon," Nandini said softly.

"Absolutely!" Shyam agreed. "Next time, we'll have even more adventures!"

Aditi smiled, looking around at her cousins, her family, and their beloved Doughnut. "This vacation has been unforgettable. Thank you, Grandma and Grandpa," she said, her voice filled with emotion. "You made it so special."

Grandma hugged Aditi tightly. "We're always here for you, sweetheart. And don't forget—family is everything."

As the night ended, Doughnut curled up on Aditi's lap for one last cuddle, and everyone drifted off to bed, knowing that no matter where they went in life, they'd always have each other, and their hearts would always be filled with the warmth of this unforgettable vacation.

Tomorrow would come, but today would forever be a cherished memory.

On the last day of their vacation, the cousins were filled with mixed emotions. They had experienced so many adventures, learned valuable lessons, and, of course, had plenty of fun with their adorable pet rabbit, Doughnut. Grandma and Grandpa's home had become the perfect getaway, and saying goodbye was never easy.

It was early in the morning, and the sun was still climbing in the sky as the cousins gathered their bags. They had packed everything the night before, but it still felt like there was so much left to say and do. Grandma was already in the kitchen, preparing one final breakfast—a spread of pancakes, fresh fruit, and the ever-popular mango pickle, which they'd all grown fond of.

"Are you all ready to go?" Grandpa called out, his voice echoing through the house. His smile was as wide as ever, though there was a little sadness in his eyes.

Doughnut hopped around in excitement, his little paws tapping on the floor. The cousins knelt down to say goodbye to their favorite furry friend. Srishti and Nandini even tried to sneak in a few extra cuddles before they left.

"I'll miss you so much, Doughnut!" Nandini said, her eyes welling up slightly. "You're the cutest bunny in the whole world."

"I think I'm going to miss you the most," Alex said, giving Doughnut one last gentle pat.

Grandma came in with a tray of their final breakfast. "I'm going to miss all of you, too," she said softly. "But don't forget, you're always welcome to visit. And remember, Doughnut will always be here to welcome you back."

They sat down to enjoy the last meal together, chatting and laughing as they reminisced about the past week. Aditi, who had been so excited about her birthday surprise, now felt a sense of sadness creeping in. She realized that it was time to go back, but the memories of this vacation would stay with her forever.

Once breakfast was finished, Grandma and Grandpa gathered the cousins for one last family toast. Grandpa raised his glass, signaling a toast to their unforgettable vacation.

"To family, fun, and all the memories we made together," Grandpa said, his voice full of warmth.

"To family," the cousins cheered, raising their glasses with smiles all around. It was a moment to remember—bittersweet, yet filled with love and happiness.

As the train tickets were handed out, the cousins said their final goodbyes to Grandma and Grandpa. They all climbed into the car for the trip to the station, and Doughnut hopped along with them, his ears twitching as if he knew the day was coming to an end.

The journey to the station was filled with one last round of stories and jokes. At the station, they boarded the train, each cousin finding their seat. They waved out the windows at Grandma and Grandpa, who stood at the platform, waving back. Doughnut gave a few excited hops, as if bidding them farewell.

"Don't worry, we'll be back soon," Aditi called out as the train began to pull away. "We'll visit you again next summer!"

With a few final waves, the train chugged down the tracks, leaving the familiar sights of Grandma and Grandpa's house behind.

As they settled into their seats, the cousins couldn't help but feel a mix of emotions. They were heading back home, but they knew that the memories of this vacation would last forever.

"We'll make sure to tell everyone about Doughnut when we get home," Riddhi said, giving a smile.

"And about the surprise birthday party for Aditi!" Shyam

added with a wink.

As the train sped along, the cousins shared one last laugh, already planning their next visit. The end of this adventure wasn't the end of their memories. The next summer, they would do it all over again—more fun, more laughter, and, of course, more time with their beloved Doughnut.

And so, the cousins traveled back to their homes, knowing that the bond they shared would remain strong, no matter how far apart they were. The vacation might be over, but the memories they made would stay with them forever, waiting for the next time they could all be together again. One by one stations came and evryone hugged each other with tears and hope in their bright eyes! Hoping to meet soon.

XX

Time For Fun

Now, it's time for FUN!

The lessons we've learned from the Earth, Fire, Water, Air, and Space are powerful, but just like those cousins, it's important to enjoy ourselves too!

Now that you've read about all the amazing adventures and lessons, here are some exciting activities for you to try. Let's bring the magic of the story into your world!

So grab your pens, pencils, and colours!!!!!!

HELP
Dougnut's friend Max to reach near him

TO DO

Make a list for your plans that you have do in this upcoming Vacations

Conclusion: The Wisdom Of The Elements

As we reach the end of this adventure, we've learned so much from the five great elements—Earth, Water, Fire, Air, and Space. Each of these elements carries a lesson that helps us understand the world and ourselves better.

From Earth, we learned that true strength lies in having deep roots. Just like the trees that stand tall in the face of storms, we too must build a strong foundation of patience, perseverance, and resilience. Water taught us to adapt and flow with life's challenges, reminding us that flexibility can often be our greatest strength. Fire ignited our passion and courage, showing us that even in the face of defeat, we must keep our spirits high and continue to pursue our dreams with determination. Air reminded us to breathe deeply, to let go of our worries, and to embrace freedom and openness. And finally, Space taught us the importance of clarity and perspective, helping us understand that sometimes, stepping back and seeing the bigger picture is the key to finding peace and happiness.

These lessons are not just stories—they are powerful teachings that we can carry with us every day. Whether we are facing difficulties, celebrating victories, or simply going about our daily lives, the wisdom of the elements will guide us toward becoming better, stronger, and happier individuals.

So, remember, just like the elements that make up our world, we too are made of resilience, adaptability, passion, freedom, and clarity. Every challenge is an opportunity to grow, and every victory is a reminder of the strength we have within.

Let's take these lessons with us, and as we continue our journey through life, let's always strive to be as strong as the Earth, as adaptable as Water, as passionate as Fire, as free as Air, and as peaceful as Space.

Gratitude Beyond Words: A Heartfelt Thank You

As I bring this book to its conclusion, I would like to express my deepest gratitude to everyone who has been a part of this journey.

First and foremost, I would like to thank my mother, whose unwavering support and inspiring ideas sparked the creation of this book. Without her encouragement and belief in my vision, this story would not have come to life.

To my family, friends, and relatives—your love, guidance, and understanding have been invaluable. Thank you for always being there for me, for your patience, and for being my source of strength.

A special thanks to my best friends, whose laughter, wisdom, and ideas have shaped not only this book but also my life in so many wonderful ways.

Lastly, to my readers—thank you for picking up this book, for diving into these stories, and for letting the lessons of the elements touch your hearts. I hope you carry them with you on your own journey and continue to grow stronger with each new lesson life brings.

This book is a tribute to everyone who has inspired me, guided me, and stood by me. I am forever grateful.

With all my love and thanks,
Avni